'You're amazing,' Marcus said huskily.

Caroline knew that she was going to spoil it, but she had to ask. 'In what way? As a doctor, a person or a woman?'

'Why do you want to know?'

'Because I need to know if I'm forgiven,' she told him with sudden recklessness.

'What for?' he asked softly. 'Using my heart as a punchball? Turning the bright path of my future into a dark alleyway?'

Caroline found herself pleading. 'I paid for it, Marcus. A thousand times over. I've so much wanted to make amends.'

'Is that so?' he challenged. 'Then show me.'

Abigail Gordon is fascinated by words, and what better way to use them than in the crafting of romance between the sexes—a state of the heart that has affected almost everyone at some time of their lives. Twice widowed, she now lives alone in a Cheshire village. Her two eldest sons have between them presented her with three delightful grandchildren, and her youngest son lives nearby.

Recent titles by the same author:

PRECIOUS OFFERINGS
OUTLOOK—PROMISING!

POLICE SURGEON

BY
ABIGAIL GORDON

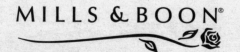

With grateful thanks to Dr D. R. Thomas
and the Stockport Police Authority

*First published in Great Britain 1999
Harlequin Mills & Boon Limited,
Eton House, 18-24 Paradise Road, Richmond, Surrey TW9 1SR*

© Abigail Gordon 1999

ISBN 0 263 81762 8

*Set in Times Roman 10½ on 11¼ pt.
03-9908-54898-D*

*Printed and bound in Spain
by Litografia Rosés S.A., Barcelona*

CHAPTER ONE

AT THE end of a warm June day the banks of the far reaches of the river that ran through the old cathedral city were dotted with those for whom the sultry night had a magic of its own.

Young lovers with hands linked and eyes locked, families where parents were allowing their little ones to stay up late because it was too hot to go to bed, and groups of teenagers, jostling and laughing as they drank out of cans.

A gang of them had stopped beside a secluded backwater and were staring down at something on the river bank. As Caroline drew near her step quickened. It was the body of a man, soaking wet and ghastly pale.

'I'm a doctor. Let me through,' she commanded with quiet authority, and as they shuffled back awkwardly she dropped to her knees beside the still figure.

There was no pulse, no heartbeat. The signs of a heart attack were there. The man was dead. Had been for some time.

Pointing to a telephone kiosk at the roadside up above, she told the gaping onlookers, 'Stay with him while I go to phone for the police and ambulance services.'

By the time she heard the simultaneous sirens of police and ambulance vehicles Caroline was surrounded by a crowd of the curious and she thought ruefully, so much for a quiet stroll after a hard day's work.

Feeling oddly restless and edgy, she'd been tempted out into the summer night like the rest of them...and had walked into this! But thankfully the police and paramedics would take over now and she could be on her way, tiredness having fallen on her like a heavy cloak.

Her departure wasn't to be as quick as she'd have liked, however. A keen young police sergeant had questions to ask, mostly routine but time-consuming nevertheless.

Eventually he said, 'I don't think we need involve you any further, Dr Croft. The police surgeon is on his way and he'll take over. Until somebody tells us otherwise, we're treating this as a suspicious death.'

Caroline nodded. 'It certainly is strange. The fact that something has brought on a heart attack isn't unusual in itself, but the fact that he's been in the water and yet was found on the bank is peculiar.'

As she left the scene of the fatality a grey Rover came gliding out of the dusk and pulled up beside the other vehicles. The face of its driver was in shadow, but she could see the shape of the head and the tilt of the chin and her heart missed a beat.

Her mouth twisted. Just because it was a magical summer night and she was lonely, it was no reason to start raking up old memories.

With an urgency in her step she pointed herself homewards to where those she loved slept the sleep of the innocent.

'The police surgeon's here now, Sarge,' a young constable announced as a tall, dark-haired figure unwound himself from the driving seat of the grey car.

As Marcus Owen stretched himself to his full height his keen glance went over the scene before him.

'What have we here?' he asked of the officer as he moved towards the inert figure on the river bank.

'Difficult to say,' the policeman said. 'We don't know how long he's been lying there, except that he was too far gone to respond to resuscitation.

'The fellow is wet through, but he wasn't in the water when he was found. A gang of youngsters came across him and a GP who was passing pronounced life extinct.'

He pointed to the man's T-shirt and shorts and the trainers on his feet. 'Looks as if he was out jogging and either collapsed and fell into the water, or maybe decided to jump in to cool off as it's a mighty warm night.

'Then, of course, he could have been pushed. At this moment it's difficult to say whether death is due to foul play or not, but there's something odd about it. We're hoping that you might be able to throw some light on the matter, Doctor.'

Marcus bent over the man and eyed him thoughtfully. The pathologist would have the final say in what had killed him, but for now the moment was his and, as in every case of a sudden or suspicious death, the police were anxious to hear what he had to say.

'There are no obvious signs of physical injury,' he told them as he made a careful examination, 'and I would say that he hadn't been in the water for more than a matter of minutes or even seconds maybe, judging from the state of his skin.'

He pointed to the man's outflung arm. 'And talking of the skin...you see the dimpling on the forearm? That's a sign that's sometimes evident when the person is an insulin user. If for any reason the dosage is too high it can cause abnormally low blood glucose, which in turn can bring on dizziness and a general feeling of weakness.

'If the man was a diabetic and had accidentally overdosed he may have felt faint and fallen into the water, managed to crawl out again, then suffered a fatal collapse of some sort.

'Or maybe he *did* jump in to cool off and the shock of the cold water on an over-heated body brought on a heart

attack. You see the blueness of the lips and the frothiness
there?

'At this moment I don't see any signs of foul play.
There's a bruise on the temple but I'd be inclined to think
it was sustained as he fell into the water or as he dragged
himself out.'

The sergeant nodded. 'Right, then, Dr Owen. I'll tell the
ambulance men to take him to the mortuary and the pathology people can follow up your theories.' He smiled.
'And no doubt come up with some of their own, just to
show they're earning their keep. In the meantime, we've
got to find out who the fellow is and break the news to his
relatives…if he has any. How old would you say he was?'

'Forty to forty-five, maybe.'

'Should have been in his prime.'

'It would appear that he was a diabetic, don't forget.'

'Yeah,' the officer agreed. 'My wife's sister is one but
she's on tablets.'

When the ambulance had left with its tragic burden, and
the representatives of law and order had gone about their
business, Marcus stood alone by the river bank with his
thoughts.

The position of police surgeon was mostly about the
down side of life. Often there were criminal overtones to
the job, but he felt that tonight's episode, depressing as it
had been, would prove to be accidental.

On the up side, the work was interesting and challenging
and he'd be keen to know if his acquaintances in the pathology department agreed with his assumptions about the
deceased jogger.

He walked back to the car with the thought of other
challenges soon to be presented coming to mind. Challenges in his career and in his private life.

As he drove slowly homewards a face from the past

came back to plague him. Was it madness that he was contemplating? he asked himself.

When Caroline Croft looked up from the notes in front of
her the surgery clock was settling onto half past ten. She
breathed a sigh of relief. For once the fortnightly practice
meeting had finished at a reasonable time. There had been
no major decisions to be made today and no long deliberations on minor matters.

All of which she was grateful for as there would be a
waiting room full of patients waiting anxiously for her to
put in an appearance. After morning surgery there would
be the usual house calls and the daily routine of the busy
GP would be well under way.

It was a procedure that she normally took in her stride
but today had started off badly, with the twins being reluctant to go to school. They both had the sniffles and had
been hankering to have the day off. After checking that
nothing really serious ailed them, Caroline had spent precious minutes pointing out that they really had to join their
classmates.

While she'd been trying to hurry them along a letter from
Stephanie had dropped onto the mat. Under normal circumstances she would have pounced on it eagerly as any word
from her sister was always welcome. But there hadn't been
time and she'd promised herself that she'd read it the moment she got to the practice, only to discover that she'd left
it on the hall table.

Both sets of circumstances wouldn't normally have bothered her if she'd had a good night's sleep, but the family
of a long-standing patient had bypassed the overnight emergency services and had rung her at home in the early hours
to ask for an urgent visit to a sixty-year-old man with severe, unremitting chest pains. Consequently she was now
feeling somewhat jaded.

Caroline had suspected a cardiac problem and by the time she'd examined the patient and subsequently put out an urgent call for an ambulance it had been half past three.

When she'd got back home the birds were already stirring. As she'd undressed wearily and eased herself back into her solitary bed, she'd wished, as she'd done countless time before, that doctoring was a nine-to-five job.

The hassle with the children and her sister's unopened letter had created a bad start to the day and now she was feeling less than her usual cheerful, efficient self.

Alison Spence, the immaculate practice manager, was getting to her feet, as were the receptionists and the nurse, but as Caroline started to do likewise Geoffrey Howard, the senior partner, motioned for her to stay in her seat.

'Don't rush off, Caroline,' he said in his flat, authoritative tones. 'There's someone I want you to meet.'

'Who?' she asked warily, thwarted in her desire to get the day's duties under way.

It was typical of Geoffrey to spring something on her when she wasn't at her best. His was a life of tranquil, elderly bachelorhood and he wasn't always in tune with the pressures that his patients and staff were under.

He had an elegant flat above the surgery where he stayed from Monday to Thursday, and on Friday mornings always left for a long weekend at his house on the coast while she was left to cope.

The mirror on the opposite wall was corroborating the fact that she was below par this morning. The image of a too-slender brunette stared back at her with shadowed violet eyes, and Caroline vowed silently that at the first chance that presented itself, she'd arrange some leave.

'I think I've solved our problem,' Geoffrey was informing her. She eyed him questioningly. 'A replacement for Robert,' he said.

'I'm not with you,' Caroline said slowly.

They'd interviewed several applicants for the vacancy of third partner in the group practice close beside the cathedral lawns.

It had come about through the sudden death of fifty-four-year-old Robert Halliday, and so far none of those seeking to fill the vacant slot had been suitable, but for Geoffrey to have made a decision without consulting her was a bit much.

As if reading her thoughts, he held up his hand in a brief placatory gesture. 'You're going to have your say, never fear. I've asked the man to meet us here at a quarter to eleven, and I suggest that if you're as impressed as I am we make a quick decision. The workload is too heavy for just the two of us, especially as I'm not available at the weekends.'

'Who is he?' she asked quickly, the vision of the full waiting room still pulling at her.

'A son of our beautiful cathedral city. Been abroad for a long time and has come home to roost. I met him through the chief constable. They've taken him on as police surgeon. Apparently he's been living in Canada and didn't want full employment when he first came back, but now he's seeking to take up the reins of general practice as well.'

'I see,' she said slowly. 'So he's intending to carry on with his work with the police?'

'I suppose so. Lots of GPs do.'

Before Caroline could tell him that she agreed whole-heartedly that they were under too much pressure, but that they needed somebody who would be fully committed to the practice without any distractions, Sue Bell, the younger of the two receptionists, appeared to say that a Dr Marcus Owen was here to see them.

'Send him in,' Geoffrey Howard commanded, unaware

that his partner had slumped back in her seat, white-faced at the announcement.

Marcus! Marcus was here! she was thinking wildly. It *had* been him in the grey Rover the other night and he was contemplating becoming the third partner in the practice! They hadn't met in years. Would he recognise her?

Her eyes flew to the mirror. Why, oh, why hadn't she spent more time on her appearance this morning, instead of just flicking the brush through her brown mop and grabbing the first blouse and skirt that came to hand?

She knew the answer, of course. It was because she was tired after a broken night and weeks of coping with one short in the practice, but wasn't it typical of life that they should meet again on a day when her usual sparkle was absent?

As the frantic thoughts raced through her mind the door opened again and Sue was ushering him in. I'm going to faint, Caroline thought. I'm going to disgrace myself by having the vapours in front of him.

But she was made of sterner stuff than that and, squaring her shoulders, she got to her feet as the two men shook hands.

She'd been aware of his eyes on her the moment he'd entered the room, and once he'd greeted Geoffrey he turned towards her.

'Caroline,' he said with flat politeness. 'How nice to meet you again.'

The senior partner was eyeing them in some astonishment. 'You two have met before?' he questioned.

Caroline found her voice. 'It was a long time ago,' she said quietly.

It was true. It was a lifetime since she and Marcus had been young lovers at medical school. They'd been in the same class at sixth form college and gone on to the same university, and during their last year they'd fallen in love.

But where his feelings had remained strong and steadfast, hers had changed because Marcus was always studying when she wanted to enjoy herself, and when she began spending her free time with blond, plausible charmer, Jamie Durant, he'd turned into a cold stranger.

Her friendship with the other youth had come about because she'd been convinced that she'd come a poor second to the career of the year's most dedicated medical student, and so she'd gravitated towards Jamie, who'd always had time for her.

The fact that he didn't know how to be serious appealed to her and she made her choice—the wrong one, as it happened. It was only later that she came to find that side of his character extremely irritating.

Jamie wasn't studying medicine. He was taking a drama course and, as she'd found to her cost in the months that followed their whirlwind marriage, everything that her smooth-talking husband did was an act. He lied and cheated constantly and often taunted her about Marcus as if he'd guessed her anguish at the terrible mistake she'd made.

When he was offered the position as entertainments officer on a cruise liner she was happy for him to take it. The further away he was the better, and as he never made any attempt to return from his sea voyages they eventually divorced.

Distressed by her youthful lack of judgement and subsequent failed marriage, Caroline steered clear of any further commitment, but always at the back of her mind was the memory of the dedicated medical student with the dark eyes and even darker hair, who'd disappeared from her life.

She tried unsuccessfully to find him and finally accepted that he must have left the country. According to what Geoffrey had just said, that appeared to have been the case.

Caroline was taking stock of Marcus as they shook hands. Gone was the slim youth of the past. In his place was a mature man with straight shoulders, trim hips and flecks of silver amongst the dark waves.

He'd been attractive in the old days, she thought, but now he was fantastic. A man in the peak of condition— mentally, if his shrewd brown gaze was anything to go by, *and* physically.

In that moment desires long dormant came to life, and as he released her hand Caroline turned away to hide her confusion.

Geoffrey was asking him to be seated and with an effort she brought her mind back to the matter on hand. What would it be like if he took the partnership? she thought dazedly. Working together? Seeing him every day? Delight? Or the extremes of frustration?

He'll be married, she told herself. Marcus is too attractive not to be. But as the conversation between the three of them progressed the only information forthcoming with regard to his private life was that he lived in a smart residential area at the other side of the cathedral.

'So, you see, this practice would be very handy for me,' he said casually, without any signs of the inner turmoil that was affecting her.

'I shall want to carry on with my work for the city police,' he went on to say. 'I've done that kind of thing before and find the role of police surgeon very interesting. I hope that it wouldn't be a problem.'

'I can't see that it would be,' Geoffrey said with unaccustomed affability. 'Do you agree, Caroline?'

She could tell that the senior partner had already made up his mind about Marcus. He'd been impressed with his qualifications and the description of the work he'd been doing abroad, and above all he was anxious to lift the burden of being a partner short. But was *she* going to be swayed so easily?

Her heart might be leaping in her breast, her legs like

jelly, but she was exhausted with the unremitting toil, and a part-time partner in poor Robert's place was the last thing she wanted.

'I'd prefer it if Dr Owen were able to give all his time to the practice,' she said quietly. 'This isn't a heavily populated city but we have a weighty workload and need complete commitment from all three full-time partners.'

Marcus surveyed her with inscrutable dark eyes. 'And that is what I'd be prepared to give,' he said with a bleak smile. 'Complete commitment. I've never offered anything less in any aspect of my life.' Which is more than can be said of you, the grimace seemed to say.

Geoffrey's mouth had pursed into the button shape that was an indication of his displeasure, but his voice was smooth enough as he pointed out, 'Dr Owen is young and agile enough to combine the two, I feel. I don't see that his work with law and order need be a problem, Caroline.'

He turned to Marcus and said with a geniality foreign to him, 'Would you leave us alone for a few moments, Dr Owen? We won't keep you long.'

Marcus nodded and as he left the room without a further glance in her direction Caroline knew what she was going to say. It would be what Geoffrey wanted to hear. That she agreed they should offer Marcus the partnership. The only trouble was that she'd be saying it for reasons that the senior partner couldn't even begin to guess at.

She'd ached to find Marcus again and the fates had at last answered her prayers. But she could see that taking Marcus into the practice would mean the end of the calm, well-ordered life she'd made for herself. The degree of contentment she'd achieved would disappear and cravings long past would come back.

Did she want that? She didn't know. Yet there was no way she could let him disappear out of her life again.

But she knew nothing about him. They'd met again as

strangers. In what light did he see her? she wondered. The successful career woman? Or a stressed-out GP? Whatever it was, she prayed that he'd approve, even though she'd expressed doubts about his participation in the running of the practice.

Her assumption that Geoffrey was willing to offer him the partnership wasn't wrong, and when Marcus came back into the room Caroline found that she was holding her breath.

Supposing he refused. After all, she hadn't been exactly welcoming. But there was no need to be concerned. Still without a glance in her direction, he accepted and Geoffrey called for Sue to bring in a bottle of sherry to toast the new arrangement. Caroline excused herself, explaining as she did so that there was a room full of patients needing her attention.

'Yes, of course, my dear,' Geoffrey agreed affably now that he'd got his own way and without any signs of making haste to assist her. 'Do, by all means, see to the ailing folk of our fair city.'

Half an hour later, as she left her consulting room to speak to the practice nurse, Marcus was coming out of Geoffrey's office, ready to depart, and as they came face to face her step faltered.

'And how is Jamie?' he asked evenly. 'I came across him a couple of years ago and he was advocating married bliss with great enthusiasm.'

Caroline felt the colour drain from her face. 'Not with me, he wasn't,' she croaked, not meeting his eyes. 'We divorced long ago.'

'And you've remarried?' he asked in the same level tones. 'I've seen you with children...twin boys.'

Her violet eyes were wide with amazement. 'You've seen me around and didn't make yourself known?'

'I'm wary of intruding where I'm not wanted. There

might have been a possessive husband tagging along behind you.'

Her face flamed. 'There's no husband,' she informed him awkwardly. 'My sons are adopted.'

There was a strange look on his face that she couldn't identify. It wasn't surprise or interest, but as if he'd retreated behind a shutter. When he didn't speak she said, rushing quickly into the silence, 'And what about you? What's been going on in your life? Did you get married?'

The shutters seemed to intensify. 'Yes, I did.'

'So she's waiting to hear your news?'

'She's dead.'

Caroline's face changed. 'Oh! I'm so sorry.'

'I married a Canadian nurse. She picked up a virus while working in a hospital out there and was dead within days,' he explained with a brevity which could have come from pain—or a desire to cut short the conversation.

'Did you love her a lot?' The intrusive question was out before she could stop it.

The blankness was still in his face as he replied, 'I loved her…yes.'

It was a strange moment. She wanted to cry, Did you love her more than you loved me? But it would have been a foolish question after all this time, and in any case she wasn't going to get the chance to voice it.

Geoffrey was coming out of his room and there was no way she wanted him to pick up on any aggravation between Marcus and herself.

With a strained smile she held out her hand again, and as Marcus took it in his she said, 'I look forward to working with you, Marcus.' And on that note of forced cordiality she went on her way.

'You don't look yourself today, Dr Croft,' Heather Sloane, the practice nurse, said as Caroline asked her to take a blood sample from a patient who was consulting her about strange sensations in her head.

'No, I'm not,' she admitted. 'I'm tired and out of sorts.' She could have added, And as well as that I've just seen a face from the past that has left me weak and wilting.

But even if she'd wanted to, there was no time for gossiping. In her consulting room was a sixty-eight-year-old who boasted she'd never had a headache in her life, but was now concerned over painless but worrying symptoms in the back of the cranium. As Caroline was aware that the woman had a history of high cholesterol, it seemed possible that there might be a thickening of the carotid arteries to the brain.

A course of non-addictive antidepressants hadn't had any effect and now, after taking a blood sample, she was about to refer the patient to a consultant for a possible brain scan.

'I keep thinking I've got a brain tumor or I'm going to have a stroke,' the woman had said, after being examined, and even though Caroline could find no signs of thickening arteries, it was clearly a case for investigation and, hopefully, eventual reassurance that the symptoms were stress-related rather than life-threatening.

Their early morning sniffles forgotten, Liam and Luke were their usual healthy selves when Caroline got home at five-thirty, and her spirits lifted when she saw two small, russet heads bent over the train set they'd had for Christmas.

At nine years old they were a constant source of joy to her. The children of an unmarried friend of hers who'd tragically died from eclampsia during childbirth, she'd adopted them at only a few weeks old and had taken time off from her career to care for them during the first years of their life.

Once they were old enough to be left she'd gone back to general practice, engaging a housekeeper to be with them while she was away. The lady in question, a motherly body by the name of Hetty Goodyear, was about to take herself off to the cinema for the evening. She said, 'They've had a glass of milk and a biscuit, Dr Croft, and the meal is in the oven.'

Caroline smiled. It was good to be home. It had been a very strange day. She'd found Marcus again, but so much water had flowed under the bridge they weren't recognisable as the same people.

For one thing they'd both been married. She foolishly, he tragically from the sound of it. She'd have given anything for him to have said that he hadn't loved his Canadian nurse, as she hadn't loved Jamie, but it hadn't seemed like that—and why should it?

She felt absurdly jealous of the woman he'd loved, yet knew she had no cause to be so. She was the one who'd broken up their relationship. She'd been young and stupid so perhaps it was excusable but *she'd* never been able to excuse herself and she'd probably never know whether *he'd* made any allowance for her youthful lack of judgement.

The red brick house that she'd bought a couple of years ago wasn't far from the cathedral itself, and she marvelled that Marcus had been living nearby and she hadn't known. When had he seen them? she wondered. Maybe it was in the nearby park as they went there almost every evening, and tonight it would be the same routine.

Stephanie's letter was lying where she'd left it in the hall, and as she eagerly devoured her sister's casual scrawl the day's uncertainties fled and happiness surfaced.

'I'm coming to your neck of the woods next week on a two-month course,' the younger girl had written from her London flat. 'Can I stay with you, Caroline? I promise I'll be good.'

Caroline hugged the letter to her. They saw each other rarely, each involved with their own lives, but the bond between them was strong and loving, and whenever they did meet up the years fell away as they laughed and gossiped together.

The older of the two by ten years, she'd never told Stephanie about Marcus as at the time of her relationship with him her sister had still been at junior school, secure in the family cocoon that had perished in later years as the result of a boating accident.

Stephanie, a bubbly blonde of twenty-six, had shown no inclination towards marriage as yet, preferring to enjoy the social scene in her own part of the capital.

When the two women were together they teased each other fondly about their vastly different lifestyles, while at the same time respecting the other's choice.

It was the height of summer and the sun was still beaming down as Caroline and the children set off for the green lawns and leisure facilities of the park.

Having discarded her blouse and skirt of earlier in the day, she was feeling more presentable in an apricot linen sundress and matching sandals, and as she raised her face to the sun's warming rays she almost stumbled over a man and a small girl, sailing a little boat on the pond provided for such pursuits.

His arm came out to steer her away from the water's edge and as her eyes flew open she gasped, 'Marcus! What are *you* doing here?'

The boys, who'd been running on in front, had come back to see what was happening and were watching curiously from a few feet away, but the small girl, engrossed in the boat, was pulling it towards her with a piece of string as if her life depended on it.

'I'm doing the same as you,' he said briefly. 'Relaxing in the park with my family.'

'Your family?' she breathed. 'The little girl is yours?'

'Yes. Her name is Hannah.'

'Who looks after her?'

The question was out before she'd thought about it.

'I do,' he said with the same brevity. 'Along with my Aunt Minette. She lives with us. She lost her husband just before my wife died and she's been fantastic. Hannah adores her.'

The boys had come closer, and as the boat became tangled in weeds near the water's edge they ran forward to help release it. The tiny girl with hair the same colour as her father's crowed with excitement.

'So it isn't long since you lost your wife?' Caroline said carefully as she eyed his small daughter.

'Hannah was one when Kirstie died. She's almost four now and she's one of the reasons I came back to England.' He looked around him, his eyes on the ancient stonework of the nearby cathedral. 'I want my daughter's roots to be in this place.'

Caroline's eyes misted. She wasn't stupid enough to think he might have come back to seek her. For one thing he'd thought that she was still married to the hateful Jamie...and for another he'd loved his wife, but she wished that he *had* come back to find her, if only to ease some of the hurt she'd done herself.

Dragging her mind back to more practical issues, she thought that it was strange that they should both be single parents, working in the same practice, but the chances of that giving them a common bond didn't look too good if Marcus continued with his present aloof attitude. Yet who could blame him? She supposed she'd asked for it.

Liam and Luke were still helping Hannah bring her boat in, and as Caroline watched their gentleness with the small girl her smile was tender.

She was always ready to allow them to let off steam but they'd been taught to be kind to others, especially younger children and animals, and the scene before her was a touching example of her training.

But they'd dallied long enough with the enigmatic widower and his small daughter, she decided. Ever since they'd met up again earlier in the day he hadn't been out of her mind, but she had the feeling that Marcus might prefer to get used to their reunion in smaller doses.

'I believe you're joining us on Monday,' she said casually, after calling the boys to her.

'Yes, that's so. Geoffrey wants me to start as soon as possible.' His eyes were on the shadows beneath her eyes but his voice was as impersonal as ever as he remarked, 'He said that you've had it tough lately.'

Caroline nodded. 'You could say that.'

'Maybe life will get better from now on,' he suggested blandly.

'I hope so,' she told him, and it wasn't just life with regard to the practice that she was thinking about. But it seemed that his mind wasn't running on the same lines as hers.

'I don't see any problem, doing my share of the workload of the practice *and* my police surgeon's duties,' he commented as if he felt that there was still censure in her attitude, but because she'd brought the point up earlier and had been sidetracked by Geoffrey Caroline wasn't going to let it pass.

'And look after a small child into the bargain?' she questioned with a half-smile.

'Yes, that, too,' he said coolly, 'but, as I've already explained, I do have some assistance from my aunt.'

'Yes, you have,' she agreed. Turning to Liam and Luke who'd moved to the water's edge again, she said, 'Come along, boys. You can help Hannah with her boat another time.'

'Can we?' they chorused, looking up at the dark-eyed man.

Marcus smiled down at them and she thought that at least he was pleasant with her sons, even if their mother was out in the cold zone.

'Of course you can,' he told them. 'If you've got boats of your own, bring them along and we'll have a boating party.'

'When?' they asked excitedly.

Marcus glanced across and met Caroline's violet gaze. 'I'll have to discuss it with your mother as she thinks that I won't have any time once I start work at the practice.'

She gave a vague smile and turned to go. Meeting Marcus twice in one day after all the years of being starved of the sight of him was too much, as was his clipped politeness.

As they walked back to the house she was thinking that life was going to be very different from now on, with him living nearby and the two of them working closely together. Suddenly, the rut that she sometimes longed to climb out of seemed a safe place to be.

When she got back there was a message on the answering machine from the husband of a patient she'd seen that morning. She'd told him to ring her at home that evening if his wife was no better, and it appeared that was the case.

Caroline frowned. When she'd seen Rowena Miles earlier in the day, the attractive young mother of two had been in excruciating pain with a neck that had been all right when she'd gone to bed the previous night but was now immovable on one side. She'd had some minor stiffness of the affected part before but today's situation was quite serious.

Suspecting arthritis or a degenerative spinal condition, Caroline had prescribed voltarol, an anti-inflammatory drug, and diazepam to relax her. But there had been other

concerns at the back of her mind as to what might be causing the problem, and she'd decided that should there be no
improvement in a few hours she had to consider the possibility of the intense pain and lack of movement being due
to bleeding at the base of the skull.

With Hetty at the cinema, she had to take the children
with her. After settling them both in the back of the car
with a comic, she drove to the Miles residence.

The patient was certainly no better when Caroline arrived
at the house, and when she told the anxious husband that
his wife would have to be admitted to hospital for tests his
alarm increased.

'I can't take the chance of missing a subdural haemorrhage or one of the rarer meningitis strains,' she told him.
'I'm going to ring around for a bed and have Rowena admitted.'

'We *are* in health care,' he said with a fraught glance at
his comatose wife.

'That should help,' she told him reassuringly. 'Can you
put a few things together for her while I make the necessary
phone calls?'

'Yes,' he agreed, calming down now that there was some
action taking place. 'I'll pack a bag and phone my mother
as soon as you've finished. She'll come over to mind the
children while we're gone.'

Caroline nodded gravely. There was always added anguish at times of illness when there were children to be
cared for. It was one of her own private nightmares that
one day she might be too ill for some reason to look after
Liam and Luke, and as the thought came it occurred to her
that Marcus must have the same concerns regarding
Hannah, but at least he had his aunt to rely on.

They had two things in common—the job and the fact
that they were both single parents—but as to the rest of it
they were poles apart because they'd changed so much.

She'd been a carefree, chestnut-haired medical student who'd got there in the end, even if her grades had been lower than his, while the Marcus she'd known in those days had been an attractive, studious youth with a droll sense of humour, a natural flair for medicine and a passion for herself that she'd carelessly cast aside.

And now she was a hard working GP and mother of two small boys. Careworn rather than carefree. Living her life with a cautious sort of wisdom born of the misery of a loveless marriage which had left her with a bruised heart and a battered ego.

He, if outward appearances were anything to go by, was a very self-contained widower, still achingly attractive but withdrawn and non-communicative when it came to others. Or maybe that state of affairs only applied to her. Maybe he was Mr Chummy with everyone else. She'd soon find out…come Monday.

CHAPTER TWO

THERE were no further sightings of Marcus and his small daughter during the remainder of that week, either in the park, in the proximity of the ancient church from where the Cathedral Practice got its name or anywhere else for that matter, and by the time Monday morning arrived the longing to see him again was a nagging ache inside Caroline.

As she came through the outer door at a quarter to nine she saw that he was already there, chatting with the rest of the staff in a friendly and relaxed manner.

He looked across at her entrance but all he had for her was a brief nod. So she still wasn't flavour of the month, she thought wryly as she hung her jacket on the peg behind the door of her consulting room.

Could it be that her rejection of him still rankled? Surely not. He'd found another love, even though the loved one was no longer around, which was more than she'd done. Hers had been a reckless, brief infatuation for which she'd paid dearly.

As she turned to venture back into Reception to face him, Caroline found Heather Sloane, the practice nurse, close on her heels.

Normally solemn-faced and industrious, the forty-year-old mother of a teenage girl was beaming, and as Caroline eyed her questioningly she said, 'Dr Owen seems as if he's going to be just what this place needs.'

'Meaning?'

Heather's smile didn't waver. 'Energetic, efficient and...dedicated.'

'I see. And you're saying that the rest of us aren't?' Caroline asked with a wry smile.

The other woman's face warmed. 'No, of course not, Dr Croft. You're the best, but you're not getting the backup that you deserve. Dr Geoffrey isn't available half the time and, although it isn't for me to comment, we're all aware that you're the one who carries the biggest burden in this place.'

Caroline sighed. The day had barely got under way and she was already involved in an in-depth discussion with the nurse about the shortcomings of the practice.

Only a few feet away stood what Heather saw as God's gift to medicine, and Caroline supposed that if his career to date had been carried out with the same amount of enthusiasm as his studies all those years ago maybe he *was* going to be the best thing that had ever happened to the Cathedral Practice.

'Yes, I'm sure you're right about him,' she agreed. Deciding that she may as well explain that they were already acquainted to avoid any gossip amongst the staff, she went on, 'We knew each other many years ago when we were both at the beginning of our careers but had lost touch until the other day when Dr Geoffrey asked him here to be interviewed regarding the vacant partnership.'

'Really! Is he married?' Heather wanted to know.

'Has been, but his wife died a couple of years ago, I believe. Dr Owen has a small daughter from the marriage.'

'Poor little mite.'

'Yes, indeed,' Caroline agreed, 'but I'd imagine that she doesn't go short of love and affection.'

Whatever had possessed her to say that? she thought irritably as Heather eyed her with growing interest. She was boosting his image like some sort of public relations guru.

Yet if the Marcus of the old days was still there inside the cool widower it would be true. His love for her had been deep and constant…and she'd cast it aside for a brief roller-coaster ride.

However, it was Monday morning. The accumulation of

the weekend's ailing population would be converging on the surgeries and she still hadn't greeted Marcus. Leaving Heather to make her way to her own domain, Caroline prepared to sally forth.

But it seemed that he was just as eager as herself to get the day under way. When she looked up he was framed in the open doorway, watching her with unreadable dark eyes.

Caroline felt her heart start to pound. She'd been hoping that his effect on her today wouldn't be as devastating as at their previous meeting, but it was worse. Every detail of him was impinging upon her consciousness—the strong jawline, the thick dark thatch above the watchful eyes and the well-cut dark suit covering the powerful but trim lines of his body.

She managed a smile. There was no way she wanted him to see how she was reacting to his presence. It would be just too humiliating if he were to realise how much he still meant to her.

'Welcome to the madhouse,' she said, holding out a slim, ringless hand. 'It's good to have you on board.'

The words were friendly enough but Caroline knew they sounded stilted, a far cry from the joyous greeting she'd have liked to have extended to him. But they were the best she could manage under the circumstances, and as he took her hand in a firm grip it seemed that Marcus was prepared to take them at face value.

'I've introduced myself to the staff,' he said with a sort of bland politeness that set her teeth on edge. 'I've familiarised myself with the layout of the place, and in particular what, I take it, is to be my room. I'm now ready to jump in at the deep end once Sue Bell's taken in the pile of patients' files that I'm going to need.'

Caroline nodded approvingly. 'That sounds fine and I'm only a step away if you need me for anything.'

He eyed her thoughtfully. 'Yes, that's true, though it may take me some time to get used to the idea.'

She looked away. What was that supposed to mean? That it made a change, having her at his beck and call?

'We'll sort out the house calls once surgery is over,' she said with practised, crisp efficiency, 'and by then Dr Geoffrey should be back from his long weekend at the coast.'

'You'll have to explain the meaning of the phrase to me some time,' he said with a rueful smile as she settled herself behind the desk. 'Weekends always seem incredibly short to me.'

'And me,' she agreed with a lightening of her heart. They were on equal ground now. Their family commitments were one thing they had in common, and amazingly she found herself saying, 'You can always bring Hannah round to my place if you want her to have the company of other children. I have a caring housekeeper who adores children. She won't mind an extra one.'

His jaw slackened for the briefest of seconds and then the barriers were up again. 'Thanks. I'll bear it in mind.'

'Sure,' she said easily, having no wish to let him think she was eager to butt into his private life. If Marcus wanted to keep her at a distance, so be it. She had no quarrel with him, far from it. She'd be happy just to be friends with this prickly stranger from her past.

But it wasn't the time for heart-searching. Their patients were waiting. It was the moment for the day to get under way, and when he departed without any further comment Caroline buzzed for her first patient to be sent in.

She'd found over the years that there were lots of tricky moments in the work of a GP, and one of them which she liked least was having to tell someone that there was no cure for the disease that ailed them.

It happened frequently with cancer patients, although with each scientific breakthrough in the treatment of the illness the numbers of the terminally ill were decreasing. But there were other blights that the frailty of the body and nature's capricious whims placed upon mankind. Blights that were not immediately fatal, but painful and incurable. Torture that had to be lived with because there was no other choice.

The woman seated opposite her was in that position. Anne Barcroft was suffering from interstitial cystitis—inflammation of the walls of the bladder. It was a nagging painful ailment which had plagued her for a long time and which was worsening.

In cases where the pain became unbearable doctors had as a last resort stretched the gradually tightening bladder walls, but it was an extremely dangerous practice as in some instances the organ had been known to burst under the strain, and Caroline would never even mention such a procedure to a patient unless the situation was desperate.

The smart, middle-aged writer had been offered a new course of treatment at the local infirmary a couple of years previously, with the warning that her vision could be affected by the drug they offered.

Weary of the constant discomfort, she'd opted to take the risk, and it was after the third of four injections that the disturbing changes in her eyesight had manifested themselves.

It had been panic stations in the urology department, with the result that an anxious consultant had ordered that the treatment cease.

The amount of the drug that she'd received had given her some relief for a period, but now the effects had worn off and she was in continual pain. Apart from medication to ease it, there was nothing that Caroline could do to help.

'I've joined a self-help group,' Anne Barcroft told her stoically.

'And has it helped?' Caroline asked.

The other woman sighed. 'Yes, inasmuch as I've discovered that there are others with the same illness who are much worse than myself. At least I don't have to wear incontinence pads, as some of those in the group do, and I'm not having to empty my bladder every half-hour as one poor woman has to, but I do wonder how I'm going to cope if it gets any worse.'

'One can hardly blame you for that,' Caroline told her patient sympathetically. 'And the awful thing is that there's nothing I can suggest in the way of even a partial cure. The illness is extremely rare. I've only ever come across it twice before you came to see me.'

'That's the story of my life,' Anne Barcroft said with a grimace. 'Nothing in it is ever uncomplicated. I'll bet I'm the only person in the city who has to filter the tap water that I use.'

Caroline smiled. She remembered how her patient had come to her some months back with severe continuing nausea which had caused them both to think that cancer of the stomach might have been present.

That had been until Anne had gone back in minute detail to the time when the problem had started, and she'd remembered that it had been then that she'd given up on a practice of years.

Having found long ago that the local tap water was hard and unpleasant to the taste, she'd started to filter all her drinking water—until some months back when she'd forgotten and had drunk straight from the tap.

It had tasted much more pleasant than before and, glad of the opportunity, she'd stopped using the filter, only to realise when she'd thought back that it had been at that time that the nausea had commenced. When she'd gone back to using the filter the dreadful sickness had gone.

'It would appear that not only did you find the drinking water unpleasant, but there must be something in it that you are allergic to—possibly the chlorine,' Caroline had said when a relieved Anne had come back to tell her the good news.

When she'd gone, with a new prescription for painkillers,

Caroline thought ruefully that Anne was one patient for whom she just couldn't get things right. The woman had cured herself of one ailment, and with regard to the other there was no cure.

At lunchtime Marcus went to a nearby restaurant for a quick lunch with Geoffrey, while Caroline ate an uninspiring sandwich in her consulting room. When the two men returned Caroline was on the point of starting her calls.

As they walked towards her across the parking area outside the practice she saw that they seemed to be on very good terms already, and she was irritated.

Was *she* going to be the outsider from now on, rather than he? Was Marcus going to charm everyone he met with his physical attractions and expertise? It looked like it but, she reasoned grimly, she had far more important things than that to concern herself with.

The job, for one thing. Until he'd put in an appearance, the boys and the practice had been her life. They still were, but a distraction in the form of the man she'd longed to meet up with again was making her see everything from different angles, and it was unsettling to say the least.

You were happy enough in your rut before he came, Caroline reminded herself as she stopped the car in front of a small bungalow not far from her own house. So why don't you stay in it and stop wishing for the moon as there are no signs of Marcus pining for *your* company.

Evelyn Archer was an eighty-year-old retired headmistress whose health had started to fail in recent months, and Caroline's visit to her that afternoon was a follow-up to the old lady's recent stay in the city's main hospital.

A diabetic with chronic valve problems of the heart and a family history of haemophilia, her health had never been good, but it hadn't stopped her from leading a full and active life.

As a carrier of the blood-related illness, she'd made a decision in her early twenties to remain unmarried as the thought of passing on haemophilia to any children she might have borne had been totally abhorrent to her.

Instead, she'd transferred her love and affection to her pupils and the children of her staff and friends, and was affectionately regarded by many.

She always enquired after Liam and Luke, interested to hear how they were getting on at school and what mischief they'd managed to get into.

Caroline had received the standard report from the hospital regarding her elderly patient's stay there and knew that her heart was in a desperate state.

And yet, when she'd let herself into the premises with the key that Evelyn kept hidden for friends and visitors such as herself, it was clear from the old woman's serene smile that she was content.

'Have you thought about going into care?' Caroline questioned gently as she sounded Evelyn's bony chest.

'Yes, I have,' she said immediately, 'and the thought of it doesn't appeal to me, although I know that I'm going to have to make a decision soon. My neighbours are very supportive but the nights are worrying. One of them has offered to sleep here but I prefer to be on my own like I've always been.'

Caroline nodded. 'I can understand that, but your heart isn't good, you know. I'm surprised they didn't have the students clustered around you when you were in hospital as its defects are quite incredible.'

Evelyn's smile was tranquil. 'They'll have their chance when I'm gone. I've left instructions for my body to be used for science.'

'Really?' This woman never ceased to amaze her. 'So you won't be having a funeral?'

'No, I'm an atheist,' she said calmly.

It was Caroline's turn to smile. If this generous, big-hearted woman was an atheist, some of the devout had better pull their socks up.

When she got back to the practice Marcus was in the nurse's room with Heather Sloane, and as she passed the open door he called across, 'Heather tells me that my predecessor used to do minor ops on Monday afternoons.'

'Er...yes...that's so,' she agreed. 'Since Robert died we've done them if and when we've had the time.'

'Yes, well, I don't see any reason why we can't go back to that routine now I'm here. I had a patient this morning who was concerned about what I'm pretty sure is a non-malignant wart on the face, and I told her to come back this afternoon to have it removed.'

'Even though you think it's non-malignant?' she questioned perversely.

He eyed her unsmilingly. 'I don't take chances on *anything*.' Including you, his dark, unwavering glance seemed to say.

'Neither do I,' she retorted, stung by his tone. 'I was merely commenting.'

The nurse was tuning in to the brief verbal crossing of swords, and without further comment Caroline went into her own room and shut the door.

But it seemed that he hadn't finished with her and seconds later he came through the connecting door between their two consulting rooms. She thought edgily that this was how it was going to be—everlastingly under each other's feet. It was an exciting thought in some aspects, but in others it was daunting, to say the least.

'Yes?' she questioned abruptly.

'You don't want me in the practice, do you?' he said grimly.

She swallowed. What was this leading up to? Was he blind?

'You'd have preferred me to stay out of sight and out of mind, wouldn't you?'

'That isn't true,' she told him, trying to keep her voice

steady. 'If I seem to be less than welcoming it's because
your disapproval of me is so obvious.'

'You're imagining it,' he said tightly as he eyed her
across the intervening space, his glance taking in the taut
slenderness of her body, the shadowed violet eyes and
glinting chestnut hair.

'If I remember rightly, when we knew each other before
you were very prone to jump to conclusions and even more
eager to jump into bed with the first gigolo that came along.
It would seem that you're doing it again.'

There was a searing pain in Caroline's chest, as if he'd
stuck a knife in it and then twisted it. He'd denied that he
disapproved of her, but he'd torn her to pieces at the same
time. She hadn't realised he disliked her so much, but the
cards were on the table and Marcus held the winning hand.
What he'd just said was true.

But why couldn't he see it in the same light as her? She'd
made one terrible mistake...and had paid for it many times
over.

Yet this cold-eyed stranger wasn't going to want to hear
about that. The hurt she'd done him all those years ago
must have been deeper than she'd known. She'd been
judged and found wanting, and he was making no bones
about informing her of the fact.

She turned her head away as tears stung her eyelids. It
wasn't a moment to show weakness. Strength was called
for if she was to hold onto some self-respect. Gripping her
hands tightly together, she gave a brittle laugh.

'Doing what again? Jumping into bed with a gigolo?'

'No. Jumping to conclusions.'

'Look, Marcus,' she said tightly, 'as far as I'm concerned, the past is past. If we're going to be working together I suggest that we keep personalities out of the relationship. It's unfortunate that we've been thrown together,
but we're going to have to make the best of it and bearing
old grudges isn't going to help.'

On that pronouncement she reached across the desk for a pile of paperwork and began to leaf through it. When she looked up again he'd gone.

Caroline took the boys for their usual romp through the park that evening with less than her normal enthusiasm. She'd felt completely deflated since her encounter with Marcus that afternoon but, as she kept telling herself, she had to get on with her life and there was no way she wanted any of her misery to wash off onto her sons.

She was going to have to put up with Marcus's antagonism during working hours, but she wasn't going to change the rest of her lifestyle because of him. And yet, as she strolled by the boating lake and children's playground and laughed with Liam and Luke, there was gloom inside her.

When she looked up Marcus and Hannah were just ahead of them, the little girl skipping along on dimpled brown legs beside the powerful figure of the man.

Caroline's step slowed. She didn't feel up to another encounter with her new colleague, but Liam and Luke weren't to know that. The moment they espied their small playmate of the previous week they went dashing towards her.

As they drew level Marcus stopped and spoke to them and then he turned, knowing that Caroline wouldn't be far behind her children.

'Hi, there,' he said in an easier tone than the one he'd used earlier in the day. 'Our respective families don't seem to have any problems with *their* relationship.'

Caroline flinched. Even in a more mellow mood he still couldn't resist a mention of their lack of rapport. Her face had tightened and, on seeing her expression, he said with a restrained sort of exasperation, 'What's wrong now?'

'Nothing,' she said flatly, as the glow faded from the bright summer evening.

'Really? Well, if that's how you look when there's nothing wrong I wouldn't like to see your expression when there is,' he commented calmly.

'How do you expect me to look when you're constantly putting me in my place?' she flared angrily.

'If you're going to be as touchy as this every time I'm around, it's going to make life difficult,' he said, without raising his voice. 'I've watched you today at the practice and seen that you're a competent and dedicated GP, admired and respected by staff and patients alike. You coped with the responsibilities and pressures of the day with a patience and resilience that I can see is an essential part of you, but when it comes to us...well...'

'Us!' she cried. 'There is no *us*. We're merely colleagues in a group practice.'

Luke had come running back and was tugging at her sleeve. 'Can we take Hannah on the slide, Mummy?' he asked.

'You'd better ask her father,' she suggested with a stiff smile.

'Yes, of course,' Marcus consented, 'but will one of you go up the steps behind her and the other one catch her at the bottom?'

Luke nodded obediently and was gone. They were left to face each other once more, but her son's intervention had brought the moment into perspective. Concealing her hurt, Caroline made an effort to guide the conversation into more impersonal channels by asking in a milder tone, 'As one colleague to another, what was your first day at the Cathedral Practice like?'

'You're interested?'

She sighed. Would they ever get around to holding a normal conversation? 'I wouldn't have asked otherwise.'

Marcus eyed her thoughtfully. 'It was memorable,' he said slowly. 'Very.'

She'd have liked to have asked in exactly what way, but

he was already answering the question and it was what she should have expected.

'Fulfilling, challenging, interesting—shall I go on?'

When she shook her head he called Hannah to him. 'It's this young lady's bedtime,' he said as he swung the little girl up in his arms. 'Aunt Min will think we've got lost.'

'Yes, of course,' she agreed. 'Until tomorrow, then.'

The words of farewell had been casually spoken but as they went their separate ways Caroline's heart was lighter because, whatever disagreements lay ahead, there'd always be the pleasure of knowing that in the practice at least he was going to be part of her tomorrows.

'Your sister's room is ready, Dr Croft,' Hetty informed her when they got back from the park. 'The sheets have been changed and I've put fresh flowers on the window-sills.'

Caroline's face lightened. 'Thanks, Hetty. I can't wait to see her.'

The older woman smiled. 'It does me good to see the two of you together. It's as if the years roll back for you.'

Caroline's answering smile was rueful. The years were rolling back in more ways than one at the moment but Hetty wasn't to know about that.

'Are there any signs of Stephanie settling down?' Hetty asked.

'Not that I know of,' Caroline replied, 'and I can't see her finding the man of her dreams amongst my few acquaintances.'

'Love comes in the strangest guises,' her housekeeper said sagely, and Caroline thought that it sometimes came twice as well, but there was no joy in that when one half of the relationship was disapproving rather than adoring.

As she tucked Liam and Luke up for the night the thought came into her mind, as it had done before, that her sister's reluctance to embrace the married state might stem from her own disastrous attempt at it. If she, Caroline, ever found out that it was so, the fiasco she'd made of her long-ago romance with Marcus would seem even more regrettable.

But, fond as they were of each other, she and Stephanie were two vastly different people. When she'd told her sister that she was adopting *two* children Stephanie had goggled at her.

'You're crazy!' she'd gasped. 'What sort of a social life will you have with two kids and your job?'

'None, I'd imagine,' she'd conceded mildly, 'but as I'm not husband-hunting and was never the social butterfly type, what does it matter?'

And it hadn't. She went out occasionally, but for the most part she was content with her lot. If she missed the magic of physical contact with the opposite sex, she accepted the loss, knowing that the shallow, unfulfilling relationship she'd had with Jamie had made her wary of committing herself again.

Yet always at the back of her mind had been the memory of one particular man who'd disappeared out of her orbit. But now everything had changed. They could be circling the galaxies together if only he could find it in himself to forgive her youthful betrayal.

When the children were asleep she went into the garden, strolling amongst the flowers in the summer dusk with the same old ache inside her.

Always on nights like this it was there, a longing for the one thing that her life lacked—a loving partner. But where before the missing one had been a nameless shadowy figure, now the image of him was so clear she felt that if she put out a hand in the darkness Marcus would be there—not having supper with his Aunt Minette while the small Hannah slept above, but here beside her, holding her close, telling her that finding her again meant as much to him as their reunion did to her.

All wishful thinking, of course, and not at all in keeping

with her usual common sense, but since when had common sense anything to do with the needs of the body—or the mind for that matter?

She turned to go back inside, smiling ruefully at her wild imaginings and knowing that the only things on offer were her solitary bed and a new medical journal which she'd promised herself she'd read before settling down for the night.

A week ago she'd been content with the routine she'd grown accustomed to, and she knew that tomorrow, in the colder light of day, her present mood would seem crazy, but at this moment, alone in the magic of a summer night, she was wishing that same safe routine a million miles away.

CHAPTER THREE

IN THE days that followed various factors emerged, one of them being a noticeable lightening of Caroline's workload, which was undoubtedly due to the arrival of Marcus Owen at the Cathedral Practice.

His contribution to the daily surgeries, house calls and minor operations, which were now back on schedule, was invaluable, and for the first time in months she felt as if she wasn't being overwhelmed by the demands of the job.

Even Alison Spence, the practice manager and a hard woman to please—especially if they were overstepping the budget—was beaming her approval, while Heather, Sue Bell and the rest of the staff were his willing slaves.

All of which was well deserved, but Caroline felt that she could do without Geoffrey's smug smile that seemed all the time to be saying, Aren't I the clever one, finding Marcus Owen?

On the morning of the practice meeting at the end of his fourth week Marcus was late.

He'd been dozing with one eye on the alarm clock when the phone had rung in the quiet of the early morning. When he'd picked it up the voice at the other end had belonged to a sergeant from the city's main police station.

'Dr Owen?'

'Yes?'

'We need you over here smartish,' the policeman had said. 'We arrested some young folk for unruly behaviour in the Cameo Club at three o'clock this morning and one of the girls has been taken ill in the cells.'

'Right. I'm on my way,' he'd told him and had proceeded to dress with all speed.

Aunt Minette had been on the landing when he'd come out of his room and he'd told the chubby-cheeked, sixty-year-old apologetically, 'I'm sorry if the phone disturbed you, Aunt Min.'

She shook her head. 'I was already up. I can't sleep on these summer mornings.'

They paused outside Hannah's door and as he opened it carefully and they surveyed the sleeping child she whispered, 'But I know someone who can.'

'Not for long, I'll bet,' Marcus said with a smile as his small daughter stirred in her sleep.

Gazing on Hannah's innocent slumbers, he was reminded of Caroline's russet-haired boys for some reason, and he thought that between them he and Caroline had three beautiful children.

Three little ones, with one mother and one father between them. A hotchpotch of relationships? Not as far as Hannah and the twins were concerned. They were totally happy. It was the adults who made life complicated.

When Marcus saw the girl at the police station her condition wiped all other thoughts from his mind. She was vomiting, and he saw that the pupils of her eyes were unequal in size in a deathly white face. Even as he noted that disturbing fact she slumped into unconsciousness, and with terse urgency he told the sergeant to phone for an ambulance.

It was clear that some time during the night she'd been injured and it had gone unobserved. The police had only shortly before become aware of the fact and it went without saying that questions were going to be asked as to who and how and when.

Marcus felt her head with careful fingers and, sure enough, there was a soft, spongy area at the side of the skull which could have been due to a blow of some kind. His face was grave. It could be a haemorrhage or something equally serious. A grim souvenir of a night out.

The sergeant was watching grimly. 'That hasn't happened since she's been in custody,' he said bluntly. 'She was in the middle of the rumpus when blows were being struck.'

'Fair enough,' Marcus told him levelly. 'She's obviously had a lot to drink as well which would have made her unsteady on her feet, but I'll still have to put in my report that she was in this state when I examined her in police custody.'

Caroline was in at the last minute for the practice meeting. She'd slept late. Stephanie had arrived the night before and the two sisters had stayed up until the early hours, talking endlessly to make up for lost time.

The younger woman had been full of her working and social life in London, and eager to know what was happening in Caroline's busy sphere. By the time they'd finally retired for the night it was as if they'd discussed every subject under the sun...with the exception of Marcus Owen's return to his roots.

To Stephanie he'd been merely one of her elder sister's friends all that time ago. Absorbed in her own youthful activities and still within the bosom of the family, she'd been only on the fringe of Caroline's student life, and after the fiasco of her marriage to Jamie Caroline had found it too painful to confide to anyone her misery and regret.

And now, with the fabric of her new relationship with Marcus so breakable, she felt the same reluctance to discuss him with her sister.

When he arrived at the practice shortly after, he said briefly to those gathered in Geoffrey's consulting room, 'I'm sorry to keep you waiting. I was called out on police business.'

It was a general comment to all those present, but it was on Caroline that his eyes were fixed. Before she'd had time to question it he was at her side, saying with quiet urgency, 'Can we have a quick word?'

'Er...yes,' she murmured, 'but it will have to be quick.' Her glance went to Geoffrey who was rustling the papers in front of him impatiently. 'Geoffrey and Alison are raring to go.'

'Even so,' he insisted, so she followed him outside into the passage.

His face was grave. 'I was called out to the police station at six o'clock this morning. A group of youngsters had been arrested for unruly behaviour at the Cameo Club in the centre of the city, and one of them was taken ill in the cells.

'I don't think the police could have been aware of how badly she'd been knocked about in the fracas. When I got there she was in a sorry state. I suspect a serious skull fracture. There was cerebrospinal bleeding from the nose and ears and she was deeply unconscious when they put her in the ambulance.'

'That's most unfortunate,' Caroline said slowly, 'but what has it got to do with me?'

'Her name is Tracey Sloane,' he said quickly, glancing over his shoulder to where the practice nurse was chatting to one of the receptionists. 'Hasn't Heather got a teenage daughter?'

'Oh!' Caroline gasped as she followed his thought processes. 'Yes, she has, and her name is Tracey. If it is her daughter, it's clear that she knows nothing of what you're telling me. She'll go crazy! Will you tell her? Or shall I?'

'I'll tell her,' he said sombrely. 'I'm the one with the first-hand information and on this occasion I wish I wasn't. It's bad enough telling her that the girl's been hurt, but what about when she hears the circumstances?'

Caroline's eyes clouded. 'I believe that Tracey's a bit of a wild one but the only thing that will matter to Heather, is that she's hurt.'

Geoffrey emerged from his consulting room and cleared his throat. The rasping noise had an ominous sound to it.

'Are we going to get started today?' he asked tartly as Marcus entered Reception and took Heather to one side.

'Can we give it a couple of minutes, Geoffrey?' Caroline asked quietly of the senior partner. 'Marcus has some distressing news for Heather.'

'Yes, of course, if that's the case,' he agreed reluctantly.

At that moment the practice nurse cried frantically, 'Not my Tracey! She told me she was staying overnight at her friend's where they were going to catch up on some schoolwork!'

Sue Bell went to stand by the stricken woman. Placing an arm around her shoulders, she said gently, 'Come along, Heather. I'll take you to her.' She added to Marcus, 'You're needed here more than I am, Dr Owen.'

When the meeting was over Caroline would have liked to have talked further with Marcus but she had to meet a consultant neurologist whom she'd asked to make a home visit to a sick child.

Consequently she was first out of the room, but as she was getting into her car on the forecourt Marcus came striding out after her.

'I know you're in a rush,' he said, 'but there's something I want to ask you before the day gets under way.'

She turned to face him. What was coming now? They were on amicable enough terms at the moment, just as long as personalities were kept on hold. That she could cope with, but anything else was like shifting sands.

He saw her expression and gave an exasperated sigh. 'I thought we'd got past the cat-and-mouse stage.'

Caroline's colour rose. He'd read her thoughts exactly. Or had he? Was he ever going to realise how much he meant to her, without her having to spell it out?

But his thought processes were running in other channels, and when she heard what they were her heart lifted.

'Hannah is four on Saturday,' he said, 'and Aunt Min

and I thought we'd have a little party for her, with you and the boys as guests...if you'll come.

'We don't know many people in the area and it worries me sometimes on her account, as well as my aunt's. *I* get to meet plenty of folk in the practice and from my work with the police, but I'd like their circle of acquaintances to be widened.'

'I'm sure that the boys would love to be part of Hannah's special day,' she said immediately, 'and so would I. Also, it will be nice to have the chance of meeting your aunt.

'Maybe you could bring her round to my place some time for a cup of tea. It can't be easy, settling into new surroundings, especially for an older person.'

It was a rash offer, considering that their domestic paths crossed so rarely. She wondered how he'd react. To her relief she saw that he was smiling, and the brief harmony between them was a precious thing.

Because of that she pushed aside the thought that the invitation to Hannah's party could have come about because she and her family were the only people he knew well enough to ask, and her answering smile had a new warmth in it as he promised, 'I'll pass the message on to Aunt Min. I'm sure she'll want to take you up on the offer. As regards the party, is half past three on Saturday afternoon OK?'

'Yes, that's fine,' she agreed. 'Can I do anything to help?'

He laughed. 'You mean, like a jelly or a blancmange or sausages on sticks? No. I've got the food organised, but if you know any games that will amuse our respective offspring they'd be welcome.'

'I'll see what I can dream up,' she promised. Then, with the urgencies of the day tugging at her, she said, 'I must go, Marcus. John will be waiting.'

He frowned. 'John?'

'John Lennox, the neurosurgeon.'

'You're on first-name terms?'

'Yes. Our paths have crossed a few times with patients and we've become friends.'

She was surprised at the way he'd been so quick to pick up on her mention of John. Surely he wasn't jealous. Whatever the reason, she supposed it wouldn't do Marcus any harm to know that her life wasn't completely devoid of acquaintances of the opposite sex. That was if he *had* given the matter a second thought.

'I see. Well, I won't delay you any further,' he said coolly and strode back into the practice building, leaving her still wondering why he'd suddenly become so prickly when she'd mentioned her friendship with the area's top neurosurgeon.

She'd met him on an occasion similar to today's—a home visit to a patient with a suspected neurological problem. This time she'd asked for his presence because the mother of the one-year-old child she wanted him to examine was suffering from some degree of agoraphobia and had been unable to face the ordeal of taking the child to hospital.

In his late thirties, hollow-cheeked, with a bushy mop of tawny hair, John had displayed a disarming lack of consequence that had appealed to her at their initial meeting, and once the consultation was over they'd chatted amicably over coffee in a nearby patisserie.

And now, if ever she had a patient needing neurological care under the auspices of the Infirmary, Caroline always referred them to John Lennox.

Sometimes he'd ring her about one of her patients and they'd have a chat. Once they'd gone for a meal on one of the rare occasions when he'd had some free time.

It was just a friendship. If John had ever shown signs of wanting more, Caroline would have backed off, but he appeared to have no more inclination than her to take it further so the relationship had continued, spasmodic and pleasant.

They arrived simultaneously outside the patient's home, and as the lace curtains at the window twitched Caroline prepared to face the anxiety inside the modest terraced house.

As they walked side by side up a short garden path John Lennox said easily, 'And so what's the story with this child, Caroline?'

'The parents have noticed poor co-ordination and there's the inability to sit up without support,' she told him. 'Little Jessica Bates sometimes goes into a sort of fit where her trunk flexes on the hips and her arms extend and abduct.'

He frowned. 'That sounds like salaam attacks. Let's hope I'm wrong. Are there any other children in the family?'

'Yes, two boys who appear to be perfectly healthy.'

Mrs Bates watched anxiously as he examined Jessica. He checked first on the child's awareness functioning, and then gave her a physical examination, paying special attention to a patch of depigmented skin on her leg.

When he'd finished his face was solemn and he told the mother gently, 'I'll need to have your daughter brought to the neurology unit for tests, Mrs Bates. Her co-ordination is more in keeping with that of a six-month-old than a child of one year. I've done what I can here but, amongst other things, I need to arrange for a computerised tomography scan—CT imaging.'

The woman was plucking at her blouse nervously and Caroline thought that Jessica's mother had more than enough on her plate with what was obviously a sick child and her own agoraphobia, without discovering that her daughter might have inherited a serious genetic illness from her. If she, Caroline, was tuning in to John Lennox's thoughts, that was how it was beginning to look.

Mrs Bates's anxiety was now mixed with dread as she listened to what he had to say, and her first reaction came quickly. 'I can't take her,' she whispered. 'Her dad will have to take the day off.'

'Just as long as somebody brings Jessica to my clinic,' he said. 'I want to see her the day after tomorrow.'

On leaving the house they stood together on the pavement, before going to their respective cars, and Caroline said, 'Am I right in thinking that the fits that the child is having are infantile spasms?'

'Yes. I think that she may have tuberous sclerosis. Did you see the rash on her face and the depigmented area of skin on the legs? Those are the signs, but I can't be sure until I've done the tests. I suspect that the mother will prove to have the illness in a mild form and has passed it on to the little girl.'

'And?'

'If I'm right we will need to start giving her immediate dosage of ACTH—adrenocorticotrophic hormone. It will stimulate the adrenal glands which could prevent any further mental damage. If it doesn't, I'm afraid that she'll end up severely handicapped.' He frowned. 'Is the mother having treatment for the agoraphobia?'

'Yes. But so far she won't venture out.'

'I see.' His face cleared as he observed her with friendly hazel eyes. 'And what's going on in your life at the moment?'

Caroline felt her colour rise. What would John Lennox say if she were to tell him that they had a new partner in the Cathedral Practice and that her thinking processes hadn't been the same since his arrival. That she was in love with him...always had been, but because he wasn't prepared to forget the smarts of the past the future wasn't looking too rosy.

'Not a lot,' she said with wry truth, 'except that we have a new partner in the practice who's also on the police surgeon rota.'

'Marcus Owen is the only police surgeon I've heard of,'

he said in slow surprise. 'Are you telling me that he's your new partner?'

'Yes. Why? Do you know him?'

'No. But from what I can gather, the boys in blue are impressed with him. He's come up with one or two surprising results in his investigations on their behalf.'

'How did it go with Lennox?' Marcus asked when she got back to the surgery.

'Fine,' she said levelly, 'although it wasn't a good day for the poor Bates family. Their little girl is having infantile spasms and John thinks the underlying cause might be tuberous sclerosis. *He* was on top form as usual.'

'Which is?' he asked casually, but there was a glint in the dark eyes meeting hers that belied his tone.

'Sheer excellence,' she said lightly, 'and he seemed to be prepared to attribute the same standards to you.'

'He doesn't know me.'

She laughed, happy to be back in Marcus's company. 'No, he doesn't but, like butter, your fame appears to be spreading.'

He was eyeing her in puzzlement. 'I'm not with you.'

'Apparently he's heard of your work with the police, which—apart from the dreadful news about Heather Sloane's daughter—is more than I have. On that thought, is there any further news about Tracey?'

'No, not yet. Sue stayed with Heather until her husband got there and then she came back here. They've moved Tracey out of Casualty and taken her to the neurosurgery unit, so your friend Lennox might be involved when he gets back.'

'Yes, maybe,' she agreed. 'He didn't mention Tracey so at that point he couldn't have been aware of what had happened.'

At some time during a busy morning Marcus had loosened his tie and rolled up the sleeves of his crisp, white shirt, and the visual impact of tanned arms covered in fine dark hair and the strong pillar of his throat, rising out of the open neckline, was playing havoc with her concentration.

Her eyes were drawn to him as if to a magnet and in that moment every other thought was blanked from her mind except the one. She craved his touch.

Apart from a couple of polite handshakes when he'd started at the practice, they'd had no bodily contact and now, illogically, in the empty passage outside their respective rooms, with staff and patients only feet away, she ached to feel his arms around her, his lips on hers.

His eyes had darkened as if the depth of her longing had communicated itself to him, but he didn't move. Instead, with a lack of logic of his own, he said quietly, 'You have the most beautiful eyes I've ever seen, Caroline, and if I'm reading the message in them aright it would appear that I'm next in line after Lennox.'

She flinched. What was that supposed to mean? That he still thought she liked to play the field? With John, who was just a friend? During working hours?

'How well you know me,' she cooed, forcing back angry tears. With a tight smile she moved towards him and when they were almost touching she reached out.

Pulling him towards her, she kissed him with defiant seductiveness, completely at odds with the tenderness that had been in her before his cutting comment.

For the first few seconds he was motionless. Then he came alive. Rising to the challenge, he returned the kiss, pressing her to him with one hand in the hollow of her back and the other tangled in the soft sweep of her hair.

It was a moment of sweet agony. Caroline felt as if they'd moved into space, that the practice and the rest of the world had ceased to exist and they were orbiting the stars.

But it wasn't meant to last—it couldn't. A phone rang

in the outer office. Alison Spence could be heard, holding forth, and her voice was getting nearer…and was that Geoffrey's heavy tread on the tiles?

There was a mutual hunger that wasn't going to be assuaged in these surroundings, she thought as they drew apart. Or was the yearning only in herself? Was Marcus just calling her bluff?

The colour had left his face, giving it a bleached look, and a pulse flickered in his neck, but his next words contradicted his ravaged appearance.

'Nice try,' he said flatly. 'I wonder what Lennox would think if he knew.'

'I've already told you that John Lennox is just a friend,' she said angrily. 'I wish I could say the same about you.'

'You have doubts on that score, do you? So, what do you see me as? The enemy?'

'No, of course not. Judge and jury maybe. Though I don't understand why when you found a woman that you loved enough to marry.'

He tensed and she felt that it wasn't because she'd taken him to task about his attitude towards her. It was because she'd mentioned the dead Kirstie. Surely the subject wasn't taboo.

If it was, she'd no chance to find out. Geoffrey *was* in the vicinity. He eyed them curiously and commented that, although she'd hadn't taken a surgery that morning, there was a patient asking for a consultation. Was she prepared to see the woman?

'Yes, of course,' Caroline agreed, bringing her mind back to practicalities. 'Who is she?'

He shook his head. 'I don't know. A newcomer, from the looks of it, who prefers to see one of her own sex.'

The woman who sat facing her some moments later was indeed a newcomer to the practice. Her notes were not to hand as she'd only just changed from another surgery in the city centre. As Caroline explained to her, it could take anything from one to two months for her records to be transferred from one doctor to another through the general practitioner committee.

'And so what can I do for you?' she asked as the elderly woman prepared to unload her fears.

'I've started with severe pains in my muscles,' the patient explained. 'They came on suddenly a couple of months ago and are getting steadily worse. I can hardly get out of bed in the morning.'

'And you say that the pain is muscular rather than in your joints?' Caroline questioned.

'Yes.'

'Are you on any kind of medication?'

'I take thyroxine for an under-active thyroid.'

She eyed the sufferer thoughtfully. 'You have all the symptoms of polymyalgia rheumatica, which is an illness that can be brought on by an under-active thyroid amongst other things.'

The woman stared at her. 'So it's not just old age?'

Caroline smiled. 'Yes and no. It is an illness that only affects older people, mainly women, but it isn't the usual creaking joints situation that the elderly have to put up with.

'I'd normally ask the practice nurse to do a blood test to check the erythcrocyte sedimentation rate, but as she isn't here today I'll do it myself. That will show the degree of inflammation present in your body, and from the result I will be able to tell if I'm right.'

She paused, and then said carefully, 'If it is polymyalgia rheumatica I'll need to put you on a course of steroids.'

Up to that point the woman had been quite calm and unworried, but at the mention of steroids she sat bolt upright in the chair.

'Oh, no! I won't start to put on lots of weight, will I?'

'Hopefully not,' Caroline assured her. 'That would only occur if you were on a very high dosage, but if I'm right you need to be on medication for the problem as soon as possible. With this kind of blood test we get a very speedy result and I'll know within a couple of days what the level of inflammation is. So come back to see me then, will you? And don't worry.'

As she watched the woman depart in a more chastened state of mind than when she'd arrived, Caroline thought that although the illness was rare she was almost certain that she was correct in her diagnosis. Treatment was imperative as the condition was sometimes associated with temporal arteritis, a condition that could cause sudden blindness.

Liam and Luke eyed her doubtfully when Caroline told them of the invitation to Hannah's party, and she had to hide a smile at their reaction.

They loved parties, but those they attended were usually the birthday celebrations of boys in their class at school or the sons of neighbours.

'We like Hannah. It would be nice to have a little sister like her,' Luke said with awkward, childish diplomacy, 'but will we be the only boys there?'

Always in tune with his twin, Liam was ready to give him backup. 'Girls don't play the sort of games that we do.'

She smiled. At nine years old they were uncomfortable in the company of the female gender, but their meeting with Hannah had been different. Because she was so small compared to themselves, they'd been protective towards her rather than embarrassed, but this was a different ball game.

'Yes, you *will* be the only boys there,' she admitted, 'but Hannah will be the only girl. There'll be just the three of you.'

The twins' faces brightened at the discovery that their standing in the junior male community wasn't threatened after all, and as their interest in the forthcoming party took an upward curve Caroline and the faithful Hetty exchanged amused glances.

With regard to her own enthusiasm for the event she had mixed feelings. When Marcus had first mentioned it, the opportunity to get to know him away from the practice had been tempting. But since then there had been his prickly attitude to John Lennox, as well as his barbed comment about her butterfly tendencies when it came to his own sex which had led to their first shattering physical contact after the long years of abstinence.

Every time Caroline thought about it her face burned. She'd instigated it. She'd responded to his taunt in anger and pent-up frustration, and the moment had got out of control—or at least it would have if they hadn't been within the restricting confines of the practice.

When they'd seen each other since then there had been no mention of it. It had been business as usual and it was only late on Friday afternoon that Marcus mentioned the party again.

'We can expect you tomorrow, then?' he said as they prepared to vacate the practice for the weekend.

'Yes, of course. The boys and I are looking forward to seeing Hannah again. We'll do everything we can to make it a happy day for her.'

His rare smile flashed out. 'Yes, I'm sure you will…and thanks for saying you'll come. As I said before, we haven't had much chance to get to know the folks around here.'

Once again the thought niggled that she and her family wouldn't have been his original choice of guests if he'd been better acquainted with the locals, but he *did* seem genuinely pleased that they were going to be there and with an answering smile she gave him the benefit of the doubt.

If Caroline had been expecting Marcus's domestic treasure to be a duplicate of her own she would have been disappointed. Where Hetty was a small bony woman with a pair

of bright blue eyes and white hair taken back in a neat coil,
Minette Townsend was plump, smooth-skinned and hadn't
a grey hair on her head.

Cool brown eyes looked her over as Marcus introduced
them, and instinctively Caroline straightened her shoulders,
while brushing back a lock of thick chestnut hair from her
face.

She groaned inwardly. Surely she wasn't seen as dubious
goods in his aunt's eyes, too? But the coolness was evap-
orating and Aunt Min's handshake was cordial enough as
the boys ran over to help a bemused Hannah unwrap the
doll they'd brought her.

Marcus had met them at the door with a white chef's hat
on his head and a plastic apron around his middle. He'd
waved a wooden spoon over them in smiling greeting and
Caroline had thought that this was a man of many facets.

When they'd been at medical school together she'd seen
only one—that of the darkly attractive student, grave and
dedicated, who had once, in a rare moment, quoted poetry
to her, beautiful lines which had been lost on the vibrant,
pleasure-loving girl that she'd been.

Since he'd joined the practice she'd seen other facets of
him. The facets of the keen police surgeon, the hard-
working GP and the unrelenting one he reserved for her.

Today she was seeing yet another side of him and it
made her heart lift. He was the welcoming host, the do-
mesticated, proud father, and as Hannah's birthday party
got under way Caroline thought wistfully that this was
Marcus at his happiest and most relaxed.

If only *she* were able to make him feel like this, but it
was more than likely that her presence was just a means to
an end as the parent of his daughter's two young guests,
and that his smiling good humour came solely from
Hannah's delight in the occasion.

Whatever the reason, she had no wish to put any blight
on the proceedings. As the afternoon progressed and they

all frolicked on the lawn at the back of the house, Caroline
felt wrapped in his good humour, and when they eventually
gathered around a table on the patio which Aunt Min and
Marcus had loaded with birthday goodies, Caroline's spirits
were just as high as anyone else's.

No sooner had they finished eating than the children were
off to play again, and Marcus went with them, leaving the
two women to finish their food at a slower pace.

It was then that Minette Townsend said casually,
'Marcus tells me that you and he were at school together
and then went on to the same medical college, Caroline.'

'Er…yes…we…did,' she replied carefully.

'It would seem that you're both from this same city,
then?' the older woman went on. Caroline nodded her
agreement, and she went on, 'It's all rather strange to me
at the moment. I've lived abroad for many years, eventually
ending up in Canada to be with Marcus and Hannah when
they lost Kirstie.'

Her eyes strayed to the man in question, who at that
moment was flat on his back, submerged beneath the bodies
of the laughing children.

'I was pleased when he decided to come back to England
to take up general practice, and to this place in particular.
I've always felt that it was pulling at him, but I suppose it
isn't surprising. His roots have always been here.'

'They're very lucky to have you,' Caroline commented,
as she thought dismally of how little she appeared to have
figured in his return to his roots.

His aunt shook her head. 'I'm the lucky one. I needed
them just as much as they needed me. My husband died
shortly after Marcus lost Kirstie. Helping out with Hannah
saved my sanity. It gave me a purpose when all purpose
seemed to have gone.'

'It must have been awful for you all,' Caroline said quietly.

'Yes, but worse for him—a busy doctor left with a small

child to care for.' Her face tightened, 'Not that he wasn't used to it.'

What was that supposed to mean? Caroline wondered. She wasn't about to find out. Liam was tugging at her arm. 'We're ready for the next game, Mummy,' he announced, and with an exaggerated groan she got to her feet.

CHAPTER FOUR

THE party finished at six o'clock, with the children grimy but content and Caroline and Marcus in a similar condition.

As the boys said goodbye to Hannah, and Aunt Min cleared away the remains of the food, the two single parents walked to the gate together.

It had been a carefree, happy afternoon and although she was hot and sticky Caroline was loth for it to end. The constraint that was usually there between herself and the tall figure at her side had been absent. He'd been relaxed and very approachable and whatever the reason for it she was grateful.

Maybe this was how he was when away from the demands of his working life, she thought as her children's nimble feet sounded on the path behind them. If that *was* the case, the more they saw of each other away from the practice, the better.

At that moment, almost as if he'd read her thoughts, Marcus stopped and, turning to face her, said easily, 'How about me taking you out for supper once our respective offspring are in bed to show my appreciation of your invaluable contribution to Hannah's party?'

Her heart leapt. Was this going to be the beginning of a real truce? When she met his eyes he was smiling, but there was a question in his dark gaze and she wondered if he was expecting her to refuse.

She might have to. There was Stephanie to consider. They saw so little of each other and her pleasure-loving sister wouldn't want to be left high and dry on a Saturday night. Hetty had already offered to be there for the boys if the two of them wanted to go out.

'I'm not sure that I can,' she said, returning the smile. 'My sister is visiting at the moment and I think she'll be expecting us to spend the evening together.'

For a moment she sensed uncertainty in him but it seemed that he wasn't to be sidetracked. 'Bring her along. Maybe we could make up a foursome if you know of a partner for her.'

Caroline stared at him. Was Marcus so anxious for her company that he was willing to dine with strangers? She doubted it. It was more likely to be a case of him wanting to finish off a happy day in a state of continuing good humour and whoever he dined with wouldn't matter all that much.

'I'll ask her,' she said slowly, 'although I don't think that Stephanie has any men friends in the area. She's lived in London for years.'

'I'll leave it with you,' he said as they followed Liam and Luke to where she'd parked her car. 'Perhaps you'll give me a ring later.'

'Yes, of course,' she agreed.

'I'd love to dine with you and your doctor friend,' Stephanie said when she heard of Marcus's suggestion, 'but who are we going to get to make up a foursome? I've no intention of playing gooseberry.'

'That isn't likely to happen,' Caroline told her wryly. 'I may have been the love of his life once, but not now. The invitation from Marcus is just his way of saying thanks for helping with his little girl's party. So it won't matter if we end up a threesome.'

But Stephanie was not to be persuaded and, rather than leave her sister on her own, Caroline was on the point of ringing Marcus to cancel the arrangement when there was an incoming call. When she picked up the receiver John Lennox's voice spoke in her ear.

'I hope I'm not interrupting anything,' he said. 'I know it's the weekend and you're off duty, but I got the results of the tests we did on little Jessica Bates this morning and I thought you'd want to know the outcome.'

'Yes, I do,' she said immediately, as the problems of the Bates family hadn't been far from her mind ever since John had seen the child earlier in the week.

'It's as I thought,' he said soberly. 'They are infantile spasms that the child is having. There's already some degree of retardation. I'm starting the treatment that I described to you when I visited her home. I only hope that it will halt the deterioration in her mental state.'

While he'd been speaking a vision of Hannah and the twins came to mind, healthy and active, careering around the garden during the afternoon, and she thought sadly that little Jessica might never achieve those simple pleasures.

'What about Tracey Sloane, the daughter of our practice nurse?' she asked before he could ring off.

They'd heard from Heather that he'd successfully operated on the girl for a subdural haematoma, but she'd still been in Intensive Care at the beginning of the weekend.

'Coming along nicely,' he said, 'but it could all have been so different if there'd been any more delay in getting her to us.'

Normally a man of few words, he was about to ring off, having said what he had to say, but with the mention of what had happened in the police station Marcus came to her mind, and she suddenly saw a solution to the problem of a partner for Stephanie.

'Are you doing anything this evening?' she asked quickly.

'Why?' he wanted to know.

'I wondered if you'd fancy making up a foursome with my sister and me and Marcus Owen.'

'The police surgeon?'

'Er…yes. He's invited me out to supper but my sister's staying with me and I don't want to leave her alone.'

'I suppose I could make myself available,' he replied. 'It

would make a change from everlastingly having my nose to the grindstone. What time would you want me to be at your place?'

'Nineish?'

'Yes. I'll see you then…and, Caroline?'

'Yes?'

'I promise not to talk shop, just as long as Owen doesn't quote crime statistics.'

She laughed. 'I'll keep you to that.'

The moment she'd replaced the receiver Caroline began to wish she'd given it some thought, before inviting John Lennox. Although the two men knew of each other they weren't acquainted, and Marcus had already read something into her relationship with the neurosurgeon that wasn't there.

However, it was too late. She'd done it now, and when she rang Marcus to confirm the arrangements she merely told him that she'd found someone to make up the four-some.

Stephanie had chosen to wear a dress of deep cornflower silk to dine out in. Bought from a London boutique, it enhanced her petite, bubbly fairness and made Caroline feel that the black silk trousersuit that she'd livened up with chunky silver jewellery was drab by comparison.

'You look very beautiful,' she told her sister generously as they awaited the arrival of the two men.

Stephanie sparkled back at her. 'And you are elegance personified.'

Caroline gave a dubious smile. Would that be how Marcus saw her? As a beautiful, elegant woman? Or would she just be a colleague he was taking out for a meal? Or the mother of the two small boys who played with his daughter? She wished she knew.

As the evening progressed it seemed to Caroline that Marcus was more taken with beauty than elegance. His eyes had warmed when he'd seen her, but then there had been a moment of tight-faced surprise when he'd been introduced to John Lennox, and after that his attention had focused on her sister. By the time they'd been shown to the table that he'd booked at a restaurant in the city centre, it was easy enough to tell who was engrossed in who.

Stephanie was at her most captivating and seemed happy enough to go along with it, and Caroline supposed she'd only herself to blame for telling her sister that there was now nothing between herself and Marcus...and for inviting John, of all people, to make up the foursome.

When he'd arrived at the house Stephanie had taken one look at the hollow-cheeked neurosurgeon and had whispered, 'Your cadaverous friend isn't my type, Caroline.' And that comment, along with Marcus's expression when he'd met John, had put the blight on the evening.

The atmosphere was cordial enough but Marcus's apparent absorption in her sister was galling to say the least, and she caught John Lennox eyeing her in puzzlement several times, as if recalling that she'd told him that she, Caroline, had been the original partner of the police surgeon.

Eventually, to her surprise, as John was no ladies' man, he set out to charm the dazzling Stephanie himself, and Marcus and she were left to resurrect what was left of the evening. A poor effort it turned out to be.

The day's earlier pleasure had been wiped out during this second meeting, and all that Caroline could think of was how much longer she was going to have to keep the set smile on her face that felt as if it were engraved there.

When they got back to the house John kept Stephanie chatting at the gate and Caroline and Marcus had the last few seconds to themselves.

He thought that she looked tired and strained in the light of a flitting moon, while for her part she was miserably aware that her contribution to the evening had been much less than memorable. But her sister had made up for any lack of effervescence on her part, and who could blame her if she found Marcus attractive?

As for John, he'd been his usual laid-back, accommodating self. She wished that it was he who made her heart beat faster and her senses leap, instead of the man who was eyeing her with a cool sort of detachment that made her want to beat her fists against his chest in protest at the assumptions he'd been so quick to make with regard to herself and the neurosurgeon.

'Thanks again for letting me share your day,' Marcus said quietly as Stephanie's laugh rang out on the night air behind them.

'I thought that it was I who'd shared yours,' she said awkwardly, resisting an insane urge to tell him that he could share everything she possessed if he'd only say the word.

He shrugged as if there was nothing further to discuss on that matter, and then, to her dismay, said, 'Your sister is excellent company. I hope that you enjoyed Lennox's attentions as much as I enjoyed hers.'

Anger flared inside her. Was he being deliberately obtuse or what? She'd told him that John was just a friend. Or was this his way of telling her that he didn't care who she latched onto as long as it wasn't him. Yet if that was the case why had he asked her out to supper?

But she knew the answer to that, didn't she? It was to offer a stilted sort of thanks for helping with Hannah's party.

'Yes, I did enjoy John's company,' she told him with cool defiance, 'but, then, I always do. If you don't mind, I'll say goodnight, Marcus. It's been a long day.' And with a wave of her hand to the two at the gate she went inside.

On Monday morning there was more good news about Tracey Sloane. She was out of Intensive Care and her parents were beginning to breathe more easily, although it would be a long time before Heather could put behind her the shock of discovering that her daughter had been in the police cells when she'd thought her safely tucked up at her friend's house.

Amongst the patients waiting to see Caroline was a thirty-year-old man whose partner had persuaded him to consult his GP about his sleeping problems.

'My girlfriend keeps telling me that she can't get any rest at night because of my heavy breathing,' he told her reluctantly, 'and as well as that I've been wondering if I have an under-active thyroid as I'm always tired. My mother and her mother had that kind of problem.'

Caroline nodded. 'Yes, I know your family history, and I'm going to take a blood sample to check that out, but although your relatives had thyroid deficiencies it's usually women who suffer from that kind of thing. However, we'll see, but first let me look in your throat.'

As she'd half expected, the man's tonsils were large and inflamed, and when she'd finished examining him she said, 'I'm going to make you an appointment to see an ear, nose and throat specialist about your tonsils and adenoids. I'm more inclined to think that any snoring problem you have lies there. Do you get a lot of sore throats?'

'Yeah, I do, but I always have.'

'Yes, well, your tonsils are in a terrible state.'

'But what about the fact that I'm always tired?' he persisted.

'That could be due to your general lifestyle—smoking, lack of fresh air and exercise or your restless sleep pattern—but let's see to your throat first. Very often when one problem is put right it solves another.'

Those confronting her during the rest of morning surgery were mainly suffering from coughs and colds and hay fever, the scourge of summer pollen, and when the last patient seated herself in front of her Caroline was grateful that the ailments she'd had to confront had been so easy to handle.

But when Amanda Prescot, a forty-year-old housewife, explained her reason for being there, Caroline knew that her gratitude had been premature.

'I was attacked on my way home from my keep-fit class last night,' she said shakily after Caroline had asked several times how she could be of assistance.

'In what way?' she questioned. 'Were you raped?'

Amanda shook her head. 'No. I managed to fight him off, but I'm bruised from head to toe.'

'Let me see,' Caroline said gently, and while the woman was removing her clothes she went on, 'Did you go to the police?'

The attack victim shook her head miserably. 'No. My husband had complained about my outfit before I went. He'd said that I was asking for trouble. But the night was so warm and we get so hot at keep-fit class that I'd just put on a pair of very brief shorts and a halter top. I daren't tell him what happened. He'd kill me!'

'Surely he'd be more concerned about your injuries than the fact that you'd had words about what you were wearing?' Caroline said quietly, as a mass of bruises were revealed on the other woman's thighs and buttocks, along with a jagged cut just below her breast.

'This must be reported, Amanda,' she said firmly but gently. 'The man can't be allowed to get away with it. One of the doctors here is a police surgeon. I'd like him to have a look at you, if you'll agree.'

Amanda shuddered. 'Will he report it?'

'If he thinks he should, yes.'

She hadn't the slightest doubt that Marcus would insist that the police were informed, and when the patient gave her reluctant permission she went to find him.

He'd finished his surgery and was having a coffee behind

Reception when she found him, but he put the cup down when he saw her expression and came towards her.

'I've got an assault victim in my consulting room,' she said quietly. 'She's cut and battered but hasn't reported it because she's scared of her husband's reaction.'

'This should have been stitched,' Marcus said when he saw the gash, 'but it needed to be done immediately. Too much time has passed to do it now. I presume your attacker had a knife?'

'I don't remember seeing one,' she whispered, 'but he must have had...and I was bare there. My top didn't cover that part of me.'

'And there was no sexual interference?'

'No.' She managed a watery smile. 'He didn't get the chance. I hadn't been to keep-fit for nothing. I saw to it that my knee came into contact with the part of his anatomy that he was relying on. I ran off as he lay gasping on the floor, but it wasn't before I'd had a battering.'

Marcus nodded gravely. 'Yes, and because of that you must report the assault. The next woman he attacks may not be so fortunate. I'm about to start my rounds but I can take you to the police station first...and if you *do* have any problems with your husband, ask him to come and have a word with Dr Croft or myself.'

'All right,' she agreed reluctantly. 'I know deep down that Bill will be more concerned about my injuries than the fact that he was right in what he said, but he'll be furious that I went out dressed as I was. He was asleep when I got in and I was huddled under the covers when he went to work this morning so he has no idea that his predictions came true.'

'I can see both points of view,' Caroline told her. 'Your husband was right to be concerned for your safety, but a woman should be able to walk the streets without being molested no matter what she's dressed in.'

Marcus was waiting at the door and as he shepherded

the attack victim through it he said in a low voice, 'Are you lunching in or out?'

'I'm going home,' she told him briefly. 'Why?'

He shrugged. 'Nothing. I'll see you later.' And he departed.

If he was suggesting a cosy chat over sandwiches and coffee, he had another think coming, she thought as she drove through the lunchtime traffic. She was still smarting from Saturday night.

The boys were at school and Stephanie had gone shopping so she and Hetty had the house to themselves. As the housekeeper put an omelette and a pot of tea in front of her, she said, 'Your sister seems very taken with Marcus Owen.'

Caroline sighed. 'Yes.'

'But I thought that you and he—'

'We do have some things in common, Hetty,' she explained wryly. 'The job, our families. But I wouldn't say that I was his favourite person. We knew each other a long time ago and he feels that I let him down.'

'And did you?'

'Yes, although I was a free agent at the time, and very young and gullible.'

'Really?' Hetty's white brows had risen and Caroline had to smile.

'Is that expression of surprise an indication that you can't visualise me ever being like that?'

'Let's just say that I've never known you as anything other than a caring mother and efficient doctor, and if that man isn't blind then he should be seeing you in the same light.'

'Maybe he does,' she agreed whimsically, 'as he's in a similar position to me. Marcus lost his wife and is bringing up his little girl on his own, but I don't think it's my present background that he finds fault with. It's old transgressions that are blocking his vision.'

'Then he needs his eyes tested!' Hetty pronounced huffily, and on that note she went to hang out the washing.

As Caroline sat, gazing into space, with the half-eaten omelette in front of her, she was wishing that he wasn't so perfect—that everything he said and did wasn't so right. He was the most self-controlled man she'd ever met.

Her face softened. Yet there had been an occasion when his armour had been pierced by passion, when they'd clung to each other like drowning souls within sight and sound of the staff and patients at the practice.

But only for the briefest space of time, she reminded herself. It hadn't taken him long to retreat behind the battlements.

It looks as if you're going to have to hang onto that crumb, she told herself. It could be the only one coming your way.

Alison Spence and Geoffrey Howard were in the process of crossing swords when she arrived back in time for afternoon surgery, and neither was willing to concede the argument.

It transpired that Geoffrey wasn't keeping to the general practice strategy of prescribing less expensive drugs whenever possible as long as there was no detriment to the patient.

The extremely efficient Alison had been checking the records and had found that in his usual autocratic manner Geoffrey had been less than sensible in some of his prescriptions, and consequently she'd brought the matter to his attention.

'You're forgetting that I'm senior partner in this practice,' he was telling her snappishly. 'I was writing out prescriptions when you were still sitting on your mother's knee!'

'Exactly!' she flung back, 'and it looks as if your thought processes are still in that period.'

That really ruffled his feathers. 'You're overstepping the mark, Ms Spence!' he said angrily.

'I don't think so,' she told him calmly. 'I'm employed to keep a check on the finances of the practice, amongst other things, and that's what I'm doing. I thought that we were all in agreement that if a cheaper drug could be prescribed with the same results as a more expensive one then we'd use it. Caroline and Marcus are keeping to that arrangement but—'

'*I'm* not?' he blustered.

'I'm afraid so.'

'Huh!' he snorted pettishly, and slammed into his consulting room.

Caroline, who'd been caught in the crossfire outside in the passage, exchanged rueful smiles with Alison. Geoffrey had always been a law unto himself, she thought as she rang for the first patient to present themselves, but maybe he'd found his match in the unrelenting practice manager.

Eileen Jackson, an energetic woman in her fifties, was one of the guides who escorted tourists around the cathedral, and her husband, Ken, of a more restrained personality, was one of the landscape gardeners there.

Caroline looked up in surprise when she came bustling into the room in response to the buzzer. 'Eileen!' she exclaimed as her glance went to the sheaf of notes for the next patient, 'I don't seem to have your records here.'

'No, you won't have, Doctor,' she said hurriedly. 'I asked the girls on Reception if I could have a quick word with you. I've come about Ken. He's booked in to see you later in the afternoon but I wanted to speak to you first.'

'I see,' she said carefully, knowing that often the interference of relatives could complicate diagnosis and treatment.

But the trim cathedral guide wasn't thinking along those lines and she said quickly, as if Ken was about to appear any second, 'He collapsed last night. Was out cold for a good five minutes, but he's insisting that it was nothing—just a faint. If I hadn't persisted he wouldn't have made an appointment to see you.

'I know what he's like. He'll play it down, make light of it,' the anxious wife said, 'but nothing like that has ever happened to him before and, as I keep telling him, there has to be a cause.'

'If your husband is going to be less than forthcoming you'd better tell me exactly what happened,' Caroline suggested, and the other woman nodded grimly.

'I was washing up and Ken was watching television when suddenly he came staggering into the kitchen with his eyes rolling and his face as white as a sheet. Then he sort of crumpled up and slid down onto the floor.'

'Did you call an ambulance?'

'Yes, but they couldn't find anything wrong with him in Casualty. They sent him home a couple of hours later, and it's because I'm not happy about it that I've persuaded him to come to see you.'

'Leave it with me,' Caroline told her reassuringly.

'Don't tell him that I've been here, will you?' Eileen pleaded. 'He'll be furious, as he hates me fussing.'

When the man in question presented himself half an hour later she saw that Ken Jackson looked his usual extremely healthy self. He was always tanned, working out in the open as he did, and today his angular brown face seemed to exude good health, but as his wife had remarked, there had to be a reason for his collapse.

She let him tell his story and was forced to conceal a smile. Eileen had been right when she'd prophesied that he'd make light of it. If Caroline hadn't known the full story she'd have thought that he'd merely stumbled and fallen.

'What exactly were you doing at the time?' she asked when he'd finished.

'I was watching a children's hospital programme. They

were operating on a toddler and there was blood every-where. Suddenly I felt that I was going to vomit and the next thing I knew I was on the kitchen floor.'

He eyed her sheepishly. 'Do you think it was the pro-gramme that did it, Doctor? I'll feel a right wimp if it was.'

Caroline leaned back in her chair. 'Yes. I think there's a strong possibility that you were affected by what you were watching. It could have been a blackout brought on by extreme emotional involvement. I've known several cases where perfectly healthy people have collapsed at the sight of blood or on hearing a graphic description of an operation, and that's what it could have been in your case. However...'

He was eyeing her uncomfortably and she went on, 'I'm not going to let it go at that. I'm going to refer you to a specialist who may decide to give you a brain scan, and in the meantime, Ken, don't drive.'

'Aw! No!' he exclaimed. 'Life won't be worth living if I can't drive!'

'If you had another attack while at the wheel there could be serious consequences for yourself and others,' she ad-monished, 'so be sensible until this matter is sorted out, will you?'

He nodded grumpily. 'It seems I haven't any choice. This is Eileen's fault. I shouldn't have come.'

Caroline's patience was wearing thin. '*She* drives, doesn't she?'

'When I let her.'

'So what's the problem?' she asked in a tone of dis-missal. Before he could answer she rang the bell to summon the next patient, who was facing terminal cancer with a great deal more serenity than Ken Jackson was displaying over his own seemingly minor problem.

She'd seen Marcus briefly before they'd started their re-spective surgeries. He'd come in on the tail end of the argument between Alison and Geoffrey, and when the contestants had departed he'd asked, 'What was all that about?'

'I'll tell you later,' she'd said, having no wish at that moment to enlarge on the fact that all was not sweetness and light in the Cathedral Practice.

The next morning Caroline awoke with Evelyn Archer, her favourite patient, on her mind, and once surgery was over she made her way to the old lady's house.

She'd seen her the previous week and hadn't been happy about her condition, but when Evelyn had told her with reluctant resignation that she was making arrangements to go into private care, Caroline had felt less uneasy about the situation.

Fishing the doorkey out of its hiding place, she gave her customary signal of three rings on the doorbell, before entering, and went in.

There was no cheery greeting this morning. When she went into the cluttered lounge she knew why. Evelyn lay dead in the big easy chair by the fire—head drooping to one side, wrinkled old face set in a peaceful white mask, spectacles hanging limply from lifeless fingers.

In those first seconds a wave of sadness swept over Caroline and then it was gone, to be replaced with relief. Often death was untimely, but not in Evelyn's case.

A divine force, or what the old lady would have preferred to believe was nature taking its course, had prevailed before she'd had to face up to losing her liberty and the independence she'd prized so highly.

After making sure that there was no life present, Caroline rang for the ambulance services and the police, then went to sit beside her.

Taking Evelyn's cold hand between her own warm palms, she stroked it gently, telling the ears that would hear no more how much she'd valued their friendship. As the words spilled forth Caroline laid her head against the old woman's bony chest and wept.

In her grief she didn't hear a footstep out in the hall, but when Marcus's voice spoke in her ear her sobbing ceased.

'Caroline!' he exclaimed. 'Whatever is going on? There's nothing more you can do for the lady.'

'I know!' she cried. 'I came in and found her like this. She was a friend as well as a patient. Yet I'm glad she's gone, Marcus. She won't have to go into care now.'

'So why all the grief?' he asked quietly.

'She was a very special person. I've known her a long time.'

'Come here,' he commanded gently, and as she laid Evelyn's hand gently back on her lap he held out his arms. Like a homing pigeon, she went into them, grateful for the comfort he was offering.

As he cradled her to him and stroked her hair, she looked up at him with tearful violet eyes and his hand became still.

The ticking of an old wooden clock on the mantelshelf was the only sound to break the silence as their glances held. Or was it her heartbeat that she could hear? She didn't know.

What she *did* know was that it was happening again— the fusing of the senses and the mind. As Marcus bent his head to hers and kissed her, gently at first and then with increasing urgency, she kissed him back. She knew that wherever her old friend might be at that moment she'd have approved.

Marcus had been driving past the old lady's house and had seen Caroline's car outside. Because he had something to ask her, he'd pulled up, expecting her to appear at any moment.

When she hadn't he'd gone in to investigate, thinking that she might need assistance with a patient, but had found that her patient was beyond help. The one in need was his partner, the woman who seemed beyond reach one moment and in the next so available that he couldn't think straight.

But he'd made that assumption once before—thinking that Caroline belonged to him—and he'd been wrong. He'd thought that he'd known the workings of her mind and heart, and he hadn't.

Marrying Kirstie had been a different experience, but even that had brought pain with it, and hurt was something he could do without.

Footsteps sounded on the path outside and he could hear voices. He put Caroline away from him with firm gentleness. His sanity was asserting itself once more.

The follow-up services had arrived and as he listened to her giving details of how she'd found her elderly patient a call came through on his mobile.

'I have to go, Caroline,' he told her. 'The police need me. There's been a suspicious death.'

'Yes, all right,' she agreed woodenly, without meeting his eyes.

Perhaps it was as well that the spell he had woven over her, here in Evelyn's house, had been broken because the happenings of Saturday night were still crystal clear in her mind. If Stephanie had said once that she thought Marcus Owen was the most interesting man she'd met in ages, she must have said it a dozen times.

The fact that he was a widower with a small child, and her sister wasn't one for encumbrances, didn't seem to bother Stephanie one bit. It was a disquieting thought.

CHAPTER FIVE

WHEN Evelyn's body had been taken away Caroline locked up the house and in a subdued frame of mind continued with her house calls, the next of which was to another elderly member of the community, but in this instance the patient was alive and improving.

William Santer, a retired train driver, had almost died from the E.coli virus the previous Christmas and was making a slow recovery because the severity of the illness had brought on a heart attack and some dysfunction of the liver.

Caroline had visited him regularly since his discharge from hospital and was keeping a close watch on his progress. There had been several cases in the area and the environmental health people had come to the surprising conclusion that it was the manure which a local farmer had used on his vegetable crops that had caused the outbreak, unlike previous occurrences when the source of contamination had been cooked meats.

Today she was pleased to see him waiting for her at the garden gate, a sure indication that he was feeling stronger. When she'd called on previous occasions he'd always been slumped in an easy chair by the fire, looking pale and ill.

'I've got it by the horns at last, Doctor,' he proclaimed with a smile.

She smiled back. 'What? The E.coli?'

'Aye. It's been calling the shots up to now, but yesterday I got up with a bit of life in me and knew I'd turned the corner.'

'You had a very nasty attack, William,' she said soberly. 'There were panic stations all round when you were fighting for your life in hospital. Especially in the butchers' shops, but as it turned out they were in the clear.'

He nodded grimly. 'Who'd have thought that buying fresh produce from a farmer could have that effect?'

'It only goes to show that in this day and age we should wash everything thoroughly before we eat it,' she commented.

He laughed, showing old yellow teeth. 'You don't mean to say that the missus has to wash the slice of boiled ham she's got for me tea?'

'I'm talking about before cooking.'

'Ah. I see.'

'Of course you see, you old tease,' she told him. 'Now, can we have you inside while I listen to that amazing heart of yours?'

'It was all for stopping, you know,' he called over his shoulder as he hobbled the path in front of her, 'but I wasn't having any. When my number's called it'll have to be for a better reason than some interfering virus.'

'The E.coli is a force to be reckoned with,' Caroline warned. 'Don't underestimate it.'

Back at the surgery Caroline found the result of the ESR blood test waiting for her. When she saw the high level of inflammation that it was showing she knew that her diagnosis of polymyalgia rheumatica had been correct, and that the patient must be contacted immediately to commence a course of the steroid drug, prednisolone, to prevent any damage to the optic nerves and subsequent blindness.

When she'd phoned her patient with the depressing news and explained that a prescription would be waiting in Reception for immediate collection, Caroline sat back in her chair and gazed thoughtfully out of the window of her consulting room.

The cathedral was bathed in afternoon sunshine. The pavements around it were crowded with casual dawdlers, shoppers and tourists, and she felt suddenly hemmed in, as if the busy, fulfilling life that she'd been content with before Marcus came back on the scene was confining her too tightly.

At that moment she saw him pull up outside in his grey Rover, and when he appeared in the doorway seconds later she saw that he looked tired and grim.

'Trouble at the nick?' she asked.

He ran a hand through the dark pelt of his hair. 'There's always trouble at the nick to varying degrees, and today was no exception, although it wasn't exactly on police premises.'

'Tell me about it.'

'I don't think you'd want to know.'

It would have been a good moment to tell him that she did want to know, that everything about him was of interest to her, but the vision of dubious dark eyes assessing her, or a cryptic comment with regard to the limitations of her past degrees of concern over him, would surely follow, and she didn't think she was up to it at that precise moment.

So she shrugged slim shoulders and told him frostily, 'Suit yourself.'

'There's no need to get uppity,' he said quietly. 'I was remembering that you've already had a distressing morning, finding Evelyn Archer dead. I'm sure you don't want to hear of any further doom and gloom.'

She smiled, the momentary annoyance disappearing because *he* was showing concern for *her*, and on a crazy impulse she said, 'I'm thinking of taking the boys to the coast one Sunday in the near future. Would you allow Hannah to come along?'

His face went blank and she wished she hadn't spoken. 'Just Hannah? What have I done wrong?'

'Er…nothing. I wasn't sure whether it would be your scene.'

'And what do you think my scene is, then?'

'I wish I knew.'

'I thought you already did,' he said with quiet irony, and then he added, making her wince, 'Will Stephanie be with you…or Lennox?'

'No. Just me and the children,' she told him coolly, wishing that she really *had* kept quiet. 'Stephanie spends her weekends with friends from the course, and John takes his elderly father out on Sundays.'

She wanted to exclaim, And he wouldn't be figuring in my plans for the day if he *was* available! But why should she have to justify her actions to Marcus?

'So it's all right if I come along whenever you decide to go?' he asked. 'Although this coming weekend I'm on call as police surgeon, which means I can't go far. From late evening on a Saturday there's usually non-stop police activity with the pubs and clubs. A sad fact of life, but nevertheless true.'

Her heart lifted. Just the mere fact that he'd asked to go with them was enough. It didn't matter if it was six months before the event took place. Suffice that he wanted to be there.

'Yes, of course it's all right, whenever we get around to it,' she told him casually. 'Bring your Aunt Min, if you want.'

He laughed. 'I don't think so. I'd imagine she'd be glad to see the back of us for a day, but Hannah would love it.'

'And what about you?' she asked, unable to resist the question.

'Oh, I'll tag along,' he said evasively, and with that she had to be satisfied.

'Guess who I came across in the city centre at lunchtime?' Stephanie said as they sat down to eat that evening.

'The Spice Girls?' said Liam.

'The Queen?' Luke suggested.

As the two women eyed them laughingly, Liam followed up with the information, 'They're singing at a pop concert.'

And Luke, not to be outdone, persisted, 'She opened the new grammar school today.'

'Neither,' Stephanie told them. 'It was someone much nicer. I'll bet your mum knows who it was.'

'Marcus?' Caroline said slowly.

'Right first time. He was coming out of the police station.'

'And?'

'And what? We had a chat and he's asked me round to his place for dinner some time.'

Caroline's spirits sank and her appetite disappeared at the same time. He hadn't mentioned seeing Stephanie when they'd talked back at the practice. Was this the moment to tell her sister that she was in love with him—had been for a long time? Stephanie, who loved her dearly, would back off, but the words were sticking in her throat for a very good reason.

There might be a degree of sexual chemistry between Marcus and herself, and along with that they worked in the same environment and had similar family commitments, but the vital spark was missing. She'd extinguished it and the Olympic flame itself wouldn't be strong enough to ignite it again.

A vision of herself as a grim-faced matron of honour, following a radiant Stephanie down the aisle, came to mind, and as she wallowed in the moment of self-pity Caroline heard voices in the hall.

'Dr Lennox is here to see you,' Hetty announced a couple of seconds later, and as Caroline eyed her in surprise John Lennox came striding into the room.

'Don't get up,' he said quickly. 'I don't want to disturb your meal. I was passing and thought I'd let you know that young Tracey Sloane is much better. I may be discharging her towards the end of next week.'

She smiled. 'That's marvellous news, John. Do her parents know?'

'Yes, of course. They're very relieved.'

'I'll bet,' Stephanie said, and he swivelled to face her.

'You're still here, then?' he questioned casually. 'Not pining for London's bright lights?'

Caroline watched the colour rise beneath her sister's fair skin. 'No, not at all.' Stephanie told him. 'It sometimes takes a change of environment to make one realise that the grass *can* be greener somewhere else.'

'Really?' he said drily as he prepared to depart. 'You must tell me about it some time.' And on that note he went.

'I didn't know that John was on regular visiting terms,' Stephanie said when he'd gone.

'He isn't,' Caroline told her. 'That's the first time he's ever been here, apart from last Saturday night when he made up the foursome.'

'Maybe you and he have got something going.'

'Maybe nothing!' she snapped. 'As I keep telling Marcus, John and I are just friends.'

When she looked up Stephanie was smiling, a bright beam on her pretty face.

'So you're not in love with either of them?'

'No. I'm not in love with anybody,' Caroline fibbed, 'and in case you haven't noticed the food's getting cold.'

When Caroline had questioned him about his activities with the police earlier that same day, Marcus hadn't been prepared to go into details mainly because, as he'd pointed out, she'd had a distressing morning, and to have had to listen to the unpleasant outlines of what he'd been involved in since their meeting at Evelyn Archer's house wouldn't have made her feel any better.

But once he'd got home and settled down for the evening he couldn't relax. He *did* need to discuss it with someone and Caroline was the obvious choice.

Not that he didn't trust his own judgement, but there were often times when as a police surgeon he came across something baffling, and the morning's happenings had been that.

His assumptions regarding the jogger on the river bank some weeks previously had proved to be correct. There had been no foul play. The man *had* become weak from an incorrect dosage of insulin, which was something that had occurred before, according to his wife.

He'd overbalanced into the river and, after managing to drag himself out, had suffered a cardiac arrest, due to the shock of his over-heated body coming into contact with the coldness of the water.

The circumstances of today's incident were by no means as easily recognisable and he felt that he was missing something.

'Looks like suicide, Doctor,' a tense inspector informed him as he'd hurried to where paramedics were bending over the body of a man lying in a deserted alleyway that ran alongside the police station. 'Though God knows why. We released him an hour ago without charging him.'

There was an empty pill bottle on the ground beside the dead man and a scattering of white tablets, but when Marcus read the label on the bottle he saw that they were merely a vitamin prescription.

'This lot won't have killed him,' he said grimly, 'but there *are* signs of poisoning. Look at the lips and mouth. There's been an intake of something that has burnt the skin. The extreme rigidity of the limbs could also be a sign of a noxious intake. What did he have in his pockets when you brought him in?'

'The usual things—keys, wallet, handkerchief,' the policeman said. 'Can't say that I remember seeing the vitamin pills, but we only asked him to empty his pockets. They could have been somewhere else on his person.' He gave a grim chuckle. 'Tell you what he did have on him, though.'

'What?' Marcus asked tightly as he examined the body.

'A bunch of horseradish.'

'Horseradish!'

'Aye. Maybe it was a trophy, something he'd picked up during the fray. It was a neighbours' squabble. The folks next door had called us out because he'd been trashing their garden. Said their trees were taking the light off his plants and because they wouldn't chop 'em down he'd climbed over the fence and started to do it himself.

'We brought him in, cautioned him and then let him go.' He looked down at the inert figure. 'But it doesn't look as if he got very far.'

'Some poisons act very quickly,' Marcus pointed out, 'but why do something so drastic over such a trivial matter?'

'He didn't see it as trivial,' the officer said. 'He was foaming at the mouth with rage.'

'Yes, well, he's foaming at the mouth for another reason now. We'll have to see what the post-mortem reveals. The coroner's office will have to be notified.'

And now, with Hannah tucked up in bed and Aunt Min in front of the television, Marcus was prowling restlessly around the house, trying to find some reason and logic in what had happened to the man in the alleyway beside the police station.

When Caroline heard his voice on the phone some minutes later her eyes widened, and her surprise increased when he said quickly, 'Are you busy?'

'Er…no. Why?' she questioned.

'Can you spare half an hour? There's something I want to discuss with you. Are the boys in bed?'

'Yes, and Hetty's in. Do you want to talk here, or shall I come to your place?'

'Let's meet halfway,' he suggested. 'It's a beautiful night for a walk.'

Her heart leapt. Was this day, which had started off so sadly when she'd found Evelyn gone, going to end on a high? A walk in the summer twilight with Marcus? What could it be that he wanted to discuss with her?

They met at the gates of the park. The man tall, with the lithe grace of the attractive male. The woman, beautiful in a slender, fine-boned way, hiding behind the protective shield of an assumed confidence which concealed the turmoil that the sight of him always roused in her.

'Thanks for coming,' he said as they strolled towards the lake, shimmering in the setting sun.

'My pleasure,' Caroline told him, and meant it more than he would ever know. She took a deep breath. 'What is it that you want to discuss?'

He'd looked happy and relaxed in those first few seconds of meeting, but now his face was sombre and she braced herself for what was to come. She reasoned that if his expression was anything to go by, it wasn't going to be something to lighten her heart…or set her pulses racing.

'I need your help,' he said, turning to face her. 'The cool, clinical thinking that is so much a part of you.'

'Connected with what?' she asked slowly, with the feeling that she might have just received a backhanded compliment.

'Connected with when I had my police surgeon's hat on earlier in the day.'

Disappointment swamped her. So he'd brought her out here on this beautiful night to talk about work. Was that all she was good for?

'You weren't prepared to discuss it earlier,' she said lightly, as if medical talk was all she'd expected of him.

'Yes, well, as I said at the time, you'd had a rough morning, but I can't get that suspicious death out of my mind. I need someone else's opinion to get a new slant on it.

'No doubt the pathology people will come up with an answer, but before they do I'd like to have some idea of my own to put forward. So far I haven't come up with anything.'

Her interest aroused in spite of the reason for him needing her presence, Caroline eyed him thoughtfully. He was always so self-contained, so efficient. She supposed she ought to be flattered that he'd even considered consulting her.

Stephanie was the one who got herself an invitation to dine at his house while she was the medical sounding-box, she thought wryly.

'So? What's the problem?' she asked quietly.

When Marcus had finished relating the incident in the alley beside the police station there was silence as she digested the facts of the strange circumstances, while admitting to herself at the same time that there *was* some degree of pleasure to be had from this unexpected conversation. He could have consulted Geoffrey, or one of his police surgeon colleagues on the rota system, but he'd sought her out instead.

'Some people like the taste of horseradish,' she said slowly, breaking into the silence. 'In its raw state it has a distinctive flavour.'

Caroline watched his head jerk up in surprise.

'What?'

'Didn't you say that the man had a bunch of horseradish on him when asked to turn out his pockets? And all his belongings would have been returned to him when he was discharged from the police station?'

'Yes,' he agreed in the same bemused fashion.

'Well, this may be a long shot—a very long shot for that matter—but you did say that it was a quarrel about their respective gardens. I seem to remember that there's a very poisonous herbaceous plant that has roots which have been mistaken for horseradish.'

'Of course!' he exclaimed. 'Monkshood, or wolfsbane as it's sometimes known. It contains the alkaloid, aconitine, which is highly toxic. It's the most poisonous plant in Britain. And you think he may have eaten it to spite the other fellow? It's an incredible thought! Yet I have a feeling that you could be right.'

He laughed low in his throat and, turning to her suddenly, hugged her to him in the excitement of the moment. 'You're amazing,' he said huskily as her head rested beneath his chin.

She knew that she was going to spoil it, but she had to ask. 'In what way? As a doctor, a person or a woman?'

It was verbal suicide but, then, she'd nothing to lose. She must have been at the bottom of his esteem for years. There was only one way to go and it was up.

'Why do you want to know?'

'Because I need to know if I'm forgiven,' she told him with sudden recklessness.

'What for?' he asked softly. 'Using my heart as a punch-ball? Turning the bright path of my future into a dark alleyway?'

His voice was flippant, mocking almost. She found herself pleading. 'I paid for it, Marcus. A thousand times over. I've so much wanted to make amends.'

'Is that so?' he challenged. 'Then show me.'

Was she hearing aright? Was this man, who boasted that he always said what he meant, asking for what she thought he was? It was an unexpected invitation, totally mesmerising. She couldn't refuse.

Raising startled violet eyes to his, she put her arms around his neck and drew his face down to hers, thinking as she did so that this was the second time that she'd taken the initiative. Was that how it was always going to be?

When their lips met he stood unyielding like that other time, willing her to light the spark—and she did, with a tenderness that would have set fire to the loins of a man of iron. Her caresses were pledges of the love she bore him. Her eyes were full of the promises of what could be if he'd let it.

At last he gave in and with a groan adored her in return. As his hands explored the soft rise of her breasts and then moved to her thighs, Caroline gave herself up to delight.

The emptiness of their reunion was being cancelled out and foundations were being laid for the future, she told herself, but it seemed that she was presuming too much. He was putting her away from him…and not with gentleness.

'What is it?' she whispered.

'You might have come up with a brilliant solution to my earlier problems,' he gritted, 'but you don't have *all* the answers.'

'What's that supposed to mean?' she flung back. 'That you think all I'm interested in is getting you into bed? Or were you trying me out to see just how big a fool I would make of myself?'

'That's something you'll have to work out for yourself,' he said flatly, and she thought that in the rays of the setting sun he looked like a bronzed forbidding god. He was taking her to task again and she couldn't bear it.

'I came to meet you because you asked me to,' she cried. '*I* wasn't the one who engineered this meeting, but it would seem that I've served my purpose…whatever it might have been…and now I'm going.' And with her back as straight as a ramrod and her chin held high she went.

'Steer clear of Dr Owen this morning,' Sue Bell, the receptionist, advised when Caroline arrived at the practice the next day. 'His usual charm is in short supply.'

'Really?'

Maybe she knew why, and then as she listened to what Sue had to say, maybe she didn't.

'He's been up half the night with his little girl who's

showing signs of having caught the chickenpox that's going around at the moment...and she's got tonsillitis with it for good measure.'

'It must have come on overnight,' Caroline said in surprise. 'He never mentioned it yesterday. Poor little Hannah. These are times when children need their mothers, but I'm sure that his aunt will do her best to fill the gap.'

'Apparently it's not so simple,' the young receptionist went on. 'The lady in question is due to go into the Infirmary this afternoon for a series of tests, which leaves him in rather a predicament.'

Caroline's eyes widened. It would seem that was something else he'd kept to himself. 'How long for?' she asked.

'Just a few days, I think. She only heard this morning and it's going to make it awkward for him with Hannah not being well enough to go to nursery school. He can't very well expect anyone else to look after her because of the infection angle.'

He could ask me, Caroline thought irritably. She was the one person who could be of use to him. Maybe not in his life, his heart, but as a port in a storm.

Hetty was strong and capable and her married niece was always available if they needed extra help. One more during daytime hours wouldn't bother her, and the boys had already had chickenpox. Marcus could drop Hannah off each morning and pick her up after afternoon surgery.

The fact that their relationship was going nowhere was of small consequence, compared to the little girl's well-being, and, ignoring Sue's warning, she went to seek him out.

He was seated behind his desk, a frown creasing his brow. When he looked up and saw her he said tightly, 'Yes, Caroline? What can I do for you?'

She perched herself on the corner of his desk and looked across at him. Last night he'd been in control while she'd been pliant and unresisting, for all the good it had done her.

Now, in the cold light of day, it was her turn, and Marcus was going to have to watch his step if he thought that snapping at her was going to get him anywhere.

But could she blame him if he was tense and uptight, with his domestic arrangements going suddenly haywire and a busy day in the practice ahead of him?

'It's what *I* can do for *you*,' she said levelly. 'I've been warned that you're a bit scratchy this morning so I'll get to the point. I believe that Hannah is poorly and that your aunt is due to go into hospital this afternoon.'

He was observing her with unreadable dark eyes. 'Yes, that's so. We had a phone call this morning to say that there's a bed for her and I won't let her turn the offer down.'

'What arrangements have you made?'

'None,' he said flatly. 'If Hannah had been well she'd have been at nursery school during the day and after that I'd have brought her back here until I'd finished surgery, but it isn't going to be so simple now that she's ill. Aunt Min wants to cancel her hospital treatment but I won't allow it.'

'So?'

'So what?'

'So I have a suggestion. Hannah can come to us. Hetty will look after her and you can pick her up each night after surgery. The boys have both had chickenpox and they'll love having her around.'

His jaw had gone slack and Caroline felt a moment's satisfaction at having taken him by surprise. But there was hurt in her too. Marcus could have asked for her help but he hadn't. She'd had to offer it and it was going to be interesting to see how he reacted to what she'd proposed.

'You mean it?' he said slowly.

'Yes, of course. I don't suppose your pride would have allowed you to ask?'

'Pride!' he hooted. 'Tell me about it! The girl that I adored saw my studies as the enemy and let it come between us. Then I got myself a wife who was more interested in her job than her family. All of which doesn't leave much room for pride.

'I'm only too grateful to take you up on the offer. To have Hannah safely tucked up at your place until Aunt Min comes home will be a weight off my mind.'

'What's wrong with your aunt?' Caroline asked, as her mind tried to take in what he'd just said about the past.

His reference to herself had hurt, though she supposed it was all she could have expected. It was his comment about the dead Kirstie which had taken her by surprise. It didn't sound much like a love match, not on his wife's side, anyway.

'Aunt Min had a cholecystectomy for the removal of gallstones shortly before we came back to these parts,' Marcus was saying. 'It was performed using the keyhole method, and I don't think it was as successful as it should have been.'

'She's had a lot of abdominal pain and the other night it was so severe and her temperature was so high that she went into an acute rigor, which only subsided as I was on the point of calling an ambulance.

'I arranged a private appointment with a consultant for the following day and he wants her in for tests. Needless to say, she's hoping that it won't mean more surgery.

'As we're both aware, there's sometimes an accumulation of bile after gallbladder treatment and it can create the problems that she's been having.'

Caroline nodded. If that was the case then his aunt might soon be home and the problem of Hannah resolved once more, but as far as she was concerned there was no hurry.

Hers was a happy household. They'd enjoy looking after

Hannah and if, by doing so, it brought Marcus more into her own social orbit, so much the better.

The only snag to that was that it would also bring him more into contact with Stephanie, and she didn't know how she'd cope with that.

'So, shall I drop Hannah off at your place after lunch?' he asked. 'On my way to the hospital with Aunt Min?'

'Yes,' she agreed. 'I'll phone Hetty and put her in the picture. And Marcus, if I were asked to give an opinion, I'd say that there's still an awful lot of pride in you…too much maybe.'

On that note she went to face the sufferers of the day, realising as she did so that in the discussion over Hannah's welfare she'd omitted to ask if the pathologist had come up with anything to give foundation to their suspicions regarding the possible aconitine poisoning.

It would have to wait until later, she decided, but there was a need to know within her. If her wild guess turned out to be right it would cause some raised eyebrows in forensic circles, but more important than that it had impressed Marcus, and to rise in his esteem would be like balm to her soul.

Sadly, though, it was as a person rather than a medic that she sought to impress him, and that day had yet to come.

CHAPTER SIX

As MARCUS drove through the evening rush hour three things were uppermost in his mind—that he'd left his fretful small daughter in a strange house, that Aunt Min had been hospitalised and that his partner had been there for him when he'd needed her. The first two thoughts were depressing. The third wasn't.

It hadn't always been the case, of course. She hadn't been there for him in the days of his youthful passion, but those miseries were long gone. Yet there was something that made him want to strike out when he was with Caroline, to make her realise how much she'd hurt him— even though she hadn't been happy either, from the sound of it.

Looking back on the deficiencies of his marriage to Kirstie, he thought that perhaps neither he nor Caroline were cut out for married bliss. Though, if that were the case, why did he keep having visions of...

He was taking the turn into the road where she lived. Her blue Volvo was outside the house. It was time for wild imaginings to cease and the basic functions of the day to resume.

There was an extra place laid at the dining table and Caroline saw that it wasn't for a child.

Hetty was hovering nearby, waiting for her reaction, and when none was forthcoming her housekeeper said, 'The little girl is really off colour. I've tucked her up in the guest room and thought that Dr Owen wouldn't need to cook himself a meal if he dined with us.'

There was no chance to answer as the doorbell rang at that moment and Caroline realised that Marcus must have been close behind her during the drive home.

'How's Hannah?' They were his first words and she sympathised with him. He'd hardly had the chance to come up for air since leaving her with Hetty, and his little girl must have been constantly in his thoughts.

There had been the usual clinics at the practice during the afternoon—antenatal, asthma—and patients requiring injections for holidays abroad, with a couple of minor operations thrown in. The three partners had been kept on the go until it had been time to face a full waiting room for afternoon surgery.

'She's poorly,' Hetty told him. 'I've put her to bed. The chickenpox doesn't seem to be bothering her. It's the tonsillitis that's the problem.'

He nodded gravely and with a glance in Caroline's direction, 'I'll go right up to her if you don't mind.'

'Yes, do,' she agreed. 'And, Marcus, Hetty has laid a place for you. Would you like to stay and eat with us?'

He paused with his foot on the bottom stair. 'I'd love to. I haven't eaten all day and I'm absolutely starving. But you don't have to do this, you know.'

'I don't have to do what?'

His smile was strained. 'Take us *both* under your wing.'

'You mean the big bird and its fledgling?' she called after him as he went bounding up the stairs.

Hetty nodded sagely. ''That's what those two are short of.'

'What?'

'A bit of spoiling. Tender loving care.'

'Hannah gets that from Aunt Min and her father,' she said with a defensive shrug.

'And where does *he* get his from?' Hetty persisted.

'I've no idea,' she retorted, and was relieved when Liam

and Luke came charging in from the garden at that moment and the matter was dropped.

She was hardly going to tell Hetty that *she'd* been prepared to offer that very thing and it had been thrown back in her face, and that their surface friendliness was exactly that—a veneer.

'Has she been taking the paracetamol syrup I left?' Marcus asked when he came downstairs again.

Hetty nodded. 'Yes, and plenty of liquids.'

'Good. Hannah certainly isn't well, but I think the next twenty-four hours should see a significant improvement in her condition.' He turned to Caroline. 'She's just gone off into a sound sleep so, if it's all right with you, I'll leave her until she wakes before I take her home.'

As if Hetty were pulling her strings, Caroline found herself saying, 'Don't disturb her, Marcus. She can stay here for the night.'

She knew that was what her housekeeper would advise, but with regard to her own feelings she wasn't so sure. But there was no doubt that it would be the best thing for Hannah, except for the fact that the little girl might not be happy to find her only parent missing when she awoke— and there was only one solution to that.

'I haven't another spare bed, but if you don't mind sleeping on the couch you can stay here with her,' Caroline said casually, as if the thought of having him under her roof wasn't the fabric that dreams are made of.

The suggestion had caught him off guard and as Caroline saw uncertainty in his dark eyes she guessed the reason for it. He'd do anything for Hannah's good, but sleeping under the same roof as herself was perhaps asking too much.

Maybe he thought she might creep in and ravish him in the middle of the night, or that she'd see it as an opportunity to bring them closer together.

If that was the case, he could think again. Pride had taken precedence over desire ever since those last spellbinding moments in his arms, and it would be a long time before she ever again took the initiative with any man.

'I do want to be there when she awakes,' he said, returning to his usual decisiveness. 'Being with strangers during the daytime is a different thing for a child than being with them at night, and so it's either I disturb her to take her home or I accept the offer of a bed for the night. I think I'm going to do that. Once I've eaten I'll go back home for my toiletries and pyjamas and some clean clothes for Hannah.'

'Yes, do that,' she agreed. 'While you're collecting your belongings I have to make a quick call.'

'A patient?'

'No, a friend.'

'Lennox?'

Caroline stared at him. 'Yes, as a matter of fact. How did you guess?'

'You've got a high colour.'

'That's not because of John Lennox!' she hooted. 'It comes from the stress of having to offer hospitality to a reluctant guest.'

He reached out and gripped her wrist. 'And how do you know that?'

'What? That you're staying here on sufferance? It's obvious from your expression.'

'So you think I'm not grateful that you're doing so much for Hannah...and myself?'

She extricated herself from his grip. 'I don't think anything, Marcus. It makes life so much simpler if one doesn't.'

They were close enough for her to see flecks of silver at his temple and tiny creases around the eyes that were certainly not the mirror of *his* soul.

He was the most clammed-up man she'd ever met, and the sad thing was that he hadn't always been like that. But, then, neither had she always been as she was now. She was

nothing like the giddy girl who'd run off with Jamie
Durant…and lived to regret it.

'I wish Kirstie could see how much you have her daughter's interests at heart,' he said quietly.

Caroline felt the breath catch in her throat. She'd only
just been condemning him for his reticence and here he
was, mentioning his past.

'*Was* she very special?' The words were choking her but
she had to ask.

'In her own way, yes.'

'And what way was that?'

Caroline knew she was pushing it. At any moment
Marcus might clam up, but something was telling her that
if she was ever going to find out anything about the woman
he'd married now was the time.

'She was quiet, shy and completely alone in the world
when I met her. I'd just come back from Europe and she
was such an undemanding sort of person to be with that
we sort of drifted towards each other.'

'You hardly make it sound like a grand passion,' she
said with a tight little laugh.

'Maybe I didn't want it to be. You know the old saying
about once bitten.'

'Yes, I do,' she snapped, 'and you don't have to keep
reminding me.'

'The meal is on the table,' Hetty called from the doorway, and that was the end of that. A brief backward look
into Marcus's life of recent years.

As she checked that her sons had washed their hands,
before eating, Caroline was thinking that she hadn't had the
chance to ask why the gentle Kirstie had been working in
the hospital where she'd picked up the virus, when she'd
had a baby to care for.

Or why, if she was such a gentle soul, had he hinted
previously that she'd put her job before Hannah and him-

MILLS & BOON®

An Important Message from The Editors of Mills & Boon®

Dear Reader,

Because you've chosen to read one of our romance novels, we'd like to say "thank you"!

And, as a **special way** to thank you, we've selected <u>two more</u> of the <u>books</u> you love so much **and** a welcome gift to send you absolutely <u>FREE!</u>

Please enjoy them with our compliments...

Tessa Shapcott

Editor, Mills & Boon

P.S. And because we value our customers we've attached something extra inside...

PEEL OFF AND PLACE INSIDE

MILLS & BOON®

With our compliments

THE
EDITORS

Yours FREE...
when you reply today

This delicate book locket is a necklace with a difference... The hinged book is decorated with a romantic floral motive and opens to reveal two oval frames for your most cherished photographs. Respond today and it's yours free.

▶ Detach along the dotted line and post this card today. No Stamp Needed ▶

Yes! Please send me my two FREE books and a welcome gift

PLACE FREE GIFT SEAL HERE

Yes! I have placed my free gift seal in the space provided above. Please send me my two free books along with my welcome gift. I understand I am under no obligation to purchase any books, as explained on the back and opposite page. I am over 18 years of age.

M9HI

Surname (Mrs/Ms/Miss/Mr) _____Initials_____

Address _____

_____

_____

_____Postcode _____

HOW THE READER SERVICE WORKS

Accepting the free books places you under no obligation to buy anything. You may keep the books and gift and return the despatch note marked "cancel". If we don't hear from you, about a month later we will send you 4 brand new books and invoice you for only £2.40* each. That's the complete price – there is no extra charge for postage and packing. You may cancel at any time, otherwise every month we'll send you 4 more books, which you may either purchase or return – the choice is yours.

*Terms and prices subject to change without notice.

The Reader Service™
FREEPOST CN81
CROYDON
CR9 3WZ

NO
STAMP
NEEDED

If this other card is missing, please write to: The Reader Service, P.O. Box 236, Croydon, CR9 3RU self? Maybe they'd needed the money, but she had a feeling that wasn't the reason.

At that moment she heard the back door slam, Stephanie was home, and for once the sound of her sister's voice wasn't pleasurable to the ear. As she greeted Marcus with obvious surprise and pleasure, Caroline turned away.

When they'd all seated themselves around the dining table Caroline felt melancholy sweep over her and knew why. With Stephanie's arrival Marcus had thrown off his sombre mood. He and the boys were getting on famously, and as her sister regaled them with an amusing account of her day on the training course at the local college everyone was laughing except herself.

When she looked up from her plate and found Marcus eyeing her thoughtfully she looked away, knowing that she was bringing gloom to the gathering.

The food was up to Hetty's usual excellent standard. Marcus's little girl was sleeping safely upstairs, and he was dining at her table. It was a moment when everything in her world ought to have been right, yet here she was wishing that the scene they presented didn't make it so obvious what her household lacked.

It needed the presence of a man—not just any man, but the one who'd come back to plague her. The man who at that moment seemed to be deriving a lot of pleasure from the company of her pretty, blonde sister.

'I've arranged to go to the cinema with an old school-friend,' Stephanie was telling him as Caroline brought her thoughts back to the present, 'and now I wish I wasn't going.'

He gave her a quizzical smile. 'Don't alter your arrangements on my account,' he said easily. 'I'm in for a busy evening. I have to go home to collect my things, stop off to visit my aunt and look after a fretful small girl into the bargain.' As Stephanie pouted in disappointment he said,

'And Caroline will be just as busy, calling on John Lennox.'

Stephanie was eyeing her curiously. 'Why him?' she wanted to know.'

'It is John's birthday,' she said quietly. 'I'm merely taking round a gift.'

'I could drop it off for you on my way to the cinema,' Stephanie offered.

'No, thanks,' she said stiffly. 'I prefer to take it myself.' If Marcus wanted to read anything into that he could do so.

When he'd gone to collect his belongings, Caroline drove to the rambling old house that John shared with his father, wondering as she did so if their friendship would have blossomed into something deeper if Marcus hadn't shown up.

It was doubtful. John was a fine doctor and a good friend but he didn't set her on fire like Marcus did, and tonight, on his birthday, she was merely stopping off for a brief visit.

They hadn't made any plans to spend the evening together and, as she'd explained to Marcus when he'd stunned her by asking if she was going to see the neurosurgeon, it hadn't been the thought of John Lennox that had been responsible for her heightened colour.

It had been due to the strain of offering her support and her home to her colleague and his daughter which had brought the flush to her cheeks, as it had seemed like only minutes since she'd vowed to steer clear of the confusion of heart and mind that she experienced when Marcus was around.

When she arrived John wasn't in and she thought edgily that she could just as easily have let Stephanie deliver the package under the circumstances, but she'd wanted to give it to him personally. As he wasn't around, his genial old father had to be the next best thing.

Marcus had called in at the hospital to see his aunt on his way back to her house, and when Caroline asked how she was coping he gave a wry smile.

'Aunt Min is enduring the tests and worrying about Hannah at the same time,' he told her, 'but the fact that she's here with you is a great relief to her.'

'So she approves of the arrangement?'

'Yes. Why not?' he replied briefly. With that she had to be content.

It was midnight when Stephanie got back from her outing and the moment Caroline heard the key in the lock she was conscious of Marcus downstairs on the couch.

Would her sister use it as an opportunity to further their acquaintance? she thought raggedly. And if she did, would he respond?

Stephanie belonged to a generation who didn't beat about the bush when they saw what they wanted. She wouldn't be dithering like a nervous virgin if she desired Marcus.

Sure enough, within seconds of her arrival there was the murmur of voices down below and the clink of pots in the kitchen. Thumping her pillow frustratedly, Caroline turned her face into it and uncharitably wished her sister back in London. At the same time she acknowledged bleakly that it took two to tango.

Hannah was restless and crotchety during the night and Caroline heard Marcus come upstairs to her twice. On both occasions she was tempted to ask if she could be of any use, but each time she told herself that the man was a GP, for heaven's sake, *and* the child's father. He wouldn't want her fussing around, and on that resolve she'd dozed off again.

But when she heard Hannah crying a third time it seemed only right, as they were guests in her house, that she should ask if she could be of assistance.

She tapped gently on the door of the spare room, and

when there was no answer she opened it slowly to reveal Marcus fast asleep in a chair beside the bed.

It was obvious that he hadn't returned to the couch after his last visit to Hannah, but at that moment his daughter's cries weren't getting through to him.

Caroline held out her arms to see if the little girl would come to her. Rewardingly, she did, and as Caroline lifted Hannah gently from under the covers Marcus stirred in his sleep.

There was stubble on his chin, his hair was tousled and with one arm flung across the arm of the chair and his legs sprawled out in front of him he looked a far cry from the crisp professional who shared her working life.

'Give Daddy a kiss,' she whispered to Hannah.

Her tears subsiding, the little girl swooped down in her arms and planted a kiss on his brow. Unable to resist, Caroline did likewise, before creeping out of the room with her young charge.

After a glass of milk and a biscuit she took the child back to bed—her own bed this time. After a few cuddles Hannah drifted back to sleep, sucking determinedly on her thumb.

As Caroline watched the little girl's lashes sweep down onto her cheeks she wondered if the departed Kirstie *was* looking down on them and, if she was, if they *did* have her approval.

Liam and Luke always came hurtling into Caroline's bed for a quick cuddle in the morning, but when they saw Hannah snuggled beside her they stopped in their tracks.

'It's all right,' she whispered. 'There's room for us all but don't be rough or you'll wake Hannah.'

It was only six o'clock but already there was birdsong in the garden and summer sunlight was dappling the ceiling above them as Hannah slept on and the boys lay quietly beside her, talking in hushed whispers.

She'd just decided that Marcus must be wondering what had happened to his daughter, and that she'd better go and inform him of her whereabouts, when there was a knock on the door. When she called out he came in.

He took in the scene at a glance and as his eyes swept over them Caroline was conscious that her nightgown was revealing and her hair a tangled chestnut mop. Thankfully, she was submerged beneath small bodies.

'Are you trying to give me a heart attack?' he asked with a tired smile. 'I woke up and Hannah was gone.'

'Correct,' she said coolly, gazing up at him from her prone position. 'I heard her crying in the night and when I went into her room you'd nodded off.'

'I see.'

His glance told her that, crowded as her bed might be, he'd noticed the nightgown, or lack of it, and for a small fragment of time she sensed that it was there again—the longing and desire that seemed to come and go in him so fleetingly.

It seemed that he'd read her thoughts because he remarked with a dry smile, 'With three small chaperons, you couldn't be safer.'

'And if they weren't here? What would it be then? Another exercise in putting me in my place?' she challenged calmly, as if being looked over by this disturbing man in her bedroom at six o'clock in the morning was nothing to get hot and bothered about.

'As the situation isn't likely to arise, you'll have to work that out for yourself,' he replied with equal easiness. Then as Hannah began to stir, 'Shall I take my daughter off your hands so that you can get dressed?'

'Is that what you'd prefer me to do?' she asked perversely.

He raised his eyes heavenwards. 'No, it isn't. What do you think I'm made of, Caroline? Iron?'

'Now, there's a thought,' she said with teasing sarcasm.

'Yes. I think you've hit the nail on the head. Iron describes you exactly…as far as I'm concerned, anyway.'

Liam and Luke were eyeing her in puzzlement. Their mother wasn't talking in her usual voice and Dr Owen wasn't smiling any more.

'What's wrong, Mummy?' Luke asked anxiously.

Caroline hugged him to her. 'Nothing, Luke. It's just that sometimes Dr Owen and I have different opinions about things.'

'What sort of things?' Liam wanted to know.

Marcus was picking a drowsy Hannah up off the bed. Their faces were only inches away and she saw a question in the man's eyes that was more urgent than that of the boys. But as the mantle of caring parents fell upon them once more the sexual chemistry disappeared, and, ruffling her son's tawny locks, she said gently, 'Oh, just things about life and…love.'

They left the house at the same time but in their separate cars. Marcus was going straight to the practice while Caroline was making a detour to drop the boys off at school.

As they went their different ways at the end of the road, last night's wild imaginings about Marcus and her sister were pushed to the back of her mind and there was a good feeling inside her.

Maybe it was because she'd been expecting Stephanie to dominate the breakfast table in the same way as she'd taken over the meal the night before, but she hadn't put in an appearance.

It had been the usual mad scramble, with lunches to pack, clean uniforms and schoolbags at the ready. With Marcus and a less fretful Hannah around, it had been even more hectic than normal.

But there'd been something nice about it, too, with the children enjoying the novelty of the situation and the grown-ups in harmony for once.

Hetty had escaped from the kitchen a couple of times and had eyed them dotingly from the doorway, and Caroline had guessed that her housekeeper was already planning what she'd wear for the wedding.

However, playing happy families didn't necessarily mean that wedding bells were going to follow. Far from it, where Marcus was concerned. Recalling their discussion of the previous night, her curiosity about his dead wife remained unabated.

The first person she saw on entering the practice was John Lennox, and as the sandy-haired consultant unrolled himself from one of the chairs in the waiting room she smiled her pleasure.

She'd been disappointed to miss him the previous night, but now he was here, wanting to thank her, no doubt.

It was typical of John that he'd found time in his busy day to do it personally, and as she beckoned him into the passage outside her consulting room he bent and gave her a swift kiss.

'Thanks for the swish golf sweater,' he said, following the kiss with a squeeze. 'I'm sorry I missed you last night. I was called out to an emergency and didn't get back until late.'

She was still in the circle of his arm when Marcus's voice spoke from behind then, and its cool, clipped tones wiped out the warmth of John's greeting.

'I'm sorry to interrupt, Dr Croft,' he was saying, 'but we have an emergency. One of the patients in your antenatal clinic has been taken ill and needs immediate assistance.'

'I have to be off, anyway,' John said. 'Duty calls for me, too. Thanks again, Caroline. We must get together soon.'

'I'd love that.' She sparkled up at him, determined not to let Marcus make her feel guilty.

'Good. I'll be in touch.'

When he'd gone striding off she said angrily, 'That was a bit much! What's wrong with the expectant mum? Surely

you could have seen to her when you saw that I was engaged!'

'She was asking for you, and "engaged" describes it
exactly,' he said. 'Cavorting about in the passage with your
boyfriend when there are patients waiting…and in any case
the antenatal clinic *is* your responsibility.'

She was really enraged now. What was the matter with
the man? Surely he wasn't jealous. She'd told him last night
that John was just a friend, but she supposed he was right.
Her patients *were* waiting, and if one of them wasn't feeling
well she'd better get it sorted out. But she wasn't letting
him get off that lightly.

'You change your moods more often than you change
your shirt,' she told him acidly. 'I thought this morning at
breakfast that there was harmony between us, if nothing
else, but you've just made me think again!' With that parting shot she swished past him into the room where a dozen
or so expectant mothers were waiting.

She saw immediately that he hadn't been exaggerating.
The girl was doubled up with pain and Heather Sloane, the
practice nurse, was bending over her.

As she hurried towards them Caroline was thinking that
it was typical that in the one instance where she'd let her
private life intrude into her work at the practice, she should
be made to appear less than caring.

But there were more important things to be concerned
about at this moment than her own pique, and Alice
McCoy, who was due to have her baby soon, was one of
them.

Valerie, her unmarried friend and the natural mother of
Liam and Luke, had died of eclampsia, and Caroline had
never forgotten the horror and tragic waste of it.

She'd never been involved with it since and didn't want
to be, but she was well aware that there was always the
risk of it in the latter months of pregnancy. As she exam-

ined Alice in the small cubicle provided, she was dreading that she might find the symptoms of it.

To her dismay they were there. Not the life-threatening signs of eclampsia, but the still very serious symptoms of PET—pre-eclamptic toxaemia—a condition that, if not treated immediately, could progress to eclampsia. Pains in the pit of the stomach, hyperactive reflexes, problems with the vision, a splitting headache—all things to bring terror to a young girl expecting her first baby.

'Have you driven here?' Caroline asked when she'd finished examining Alice.

'No,' she said tearfully. 'We haven't got a car.'

'It wouldn't have made any odds if you had,' she told her. 'You're not fit to drive. I'm going to ring for an ambulance to take you to the maternity unit at St Xavier's Hospital.'

'It's serious, isn't it?' Alice quavered.

'Yes. I'm afraid it is,' Caroline told her gently, 'but we've caught it in time. How long have you been feeling like this?'

'It started at the beginning of the week. I thought it was a stomach bug I'd picked up, but when I started jerking about and couldn't see properly I became worried. Knowing that it was your clinic this morning, I came straight here.'

'Yes. You did well to see me quickly,' Caroline said reassuringly, thinking that it was fortunate that she hadn't delayed any longer.

'What will they do?' the expectant mother asked fearfully.

'Bed rest and something to bring your blood pressure down.'

Alice smiled in tearful relief. 'Oh! Is that all?'

'More or less. It will depend on how quickly you react to treatment. The main aim of the doctors who attend you at St Xavier's will be to stop your condition becoming eclampsia. Having got to grips with it so soon, I don't think there's any risk.'

Once Alice had been whisked away in the ambulance there was a subdued atmosphere amongst the rest of the mothers-to-be. Even though they were all pronounced fit and well, the gloom persisted until the weekly clinic was over.

'I suppose that they were all thinking that it could have been them,' Heather said as she cleared away afterwards, and with thoughts of Valerie still uppermost in her mind Caroline nodded sombrely.

After her meeting with John in the passage and the subsequent terse words between Marcus and herself which had sent her rushing into the clinic, Caroline didn't go into her own room until it was almost lunchtime. When she did so she stopped short in surprise.

There was a large bouquet of flowers on her desk—a profusion of stargazer lilies, pale pink roses and white carnations. As she walked slowly across to read the card she was thinking that John must have been in there, before seating himself in the waiting room.

But the writing on the card wasn't in his indifferent scrawl. It was written in a bold, clear hand and the message was, 'Thank you for everything, Caroline. I owe you. Marcus.'

As the scent of the lilies drifted upwards she shook her head in disbelief. He must have called in at the florist on his way to the practice. The flowers were beautiful, chosen with care, but the card was so brief and unromantic it just wasn't true!

She supposed she could pretend that 'I owe you' was 'I love you,' but who would she be kidding?

However, manners demanded that she must thank him. Before going out for a sandwich, she knocked on the door of his room. Getting no reply, she went in.

There was a note on his desk addressed to no one in particular. It said, 'Have gone to see Hannah. Back soon.'

Her face softened and she immediately forgave him for his earlier crabbiness. He'd gone dashing off to see his daughter without any lunch and had found the time to buy her flowers at the start of his busy morning. He was some man! But not hers, unfortunately.

'Thank you for the flowers,' she said softly when he came dashing back at the end of the lunch hour. 'How did you know that I adore stargazer lilies?'

He was smiling and it was actually reaching his eyes, those dark orbs that gave nothing away yet seemed to have no difficulty seeing into *her* mind.

'It was just an inspired guess. A striking flower for a striking woman.'

Caroline could feel her cheeks starting to burn. She was behaving like a stargazer herself, or a moonstruck adolescent. But a compliment from Marcus was a rare thing and its unexpectedness had thrown her into confusion.

With the functions of the practice going on around them, maybe it was time to change the subject.

'How's Hannah?' she asked.

'Much better,' he said with the smile still in evidence. 'She'd had some lunch and Hetty did me a quick sandwich. That woman is a gem!'

'Yes, she is,' she agreed warmly. 'I'd be lost without her.'

'The same as I would be without Aunt Min,' he said gravely, 'and with that thought comes another. She's getting older and more tired and I feel that, much as she loves helping with Hannah, it's getting too much for her. I think the time is coming when I'll have to make different arrangements.'

'And what are they likely to be?' she asked quickly, achingly aware that every aspect of his life was important to her.

'I'm not sure at the moment. I was merely making an observation,' he said calmly, and on that note they separated, Caroline to the weekly heart clinic and Marcus to answer a call for an urgent visit.

CHAPTER SEVEN

MARCUS and Hannah stayed with them for three days. They could have returned home earlier as the little girl was soon much better, but for some reason no one seemed to want to push the matter.

Caroline certainly didn't, and as far as Hetty was concerned they could have stayed for ever. The same applied to Liam and Luke, and Caroline thought a few times that it didn't matter how good she was at wielding a cricket bat or baiting a hook, it just didn't have the same kind of appeal as when the action was performed by one of their own sex.

On one occasion in particular, as they'd all played in the park in the early evening, she'd been especially conscious of their two small, russet heads and the darker thatch of the man, bent intently over the little sailing boat which had come to grief in the pond. She'd thought painfully that she mustn't let the boys get too fond of Marcus.

For all she knew he might just be humouring them, spending time with them as part of his function as her guest, and yet she gave the same attention to Hannah, didn't she? It was a pleasure to have her around.

Hannah had been there beside her at that moment, playing contentedly with one of her dolls, too young to be hurt if this strange friendship petered out as it very well might whereas *her* children could be taking Marcus's presence in their lives too much for granted and be hurt in the process.

Should she warn him not to get too close to them? Or should she let them have the pleasure of being with him for as long as the opportunity was there, and risk coping with their disappointment if he withdrew himself from their lives?

Her doubts and heart-searchings were pushed to one side when on the third morning he said over breakfast, 'I feel that we've enjoyed your hospitality for long enough, Caroline. We'll go back home this evening.

'Hannah is well again and Aunt Min is to be discharged tomorrow. I've spoken to the consultant and the tests have shown that there was still a gallstone there and it *was* an accumulation of trapped bile that was causing the rigors and general discomfort.'

'You don't *have* to rush back,' she said quickly, desperate to hold onto the brief idyll now that it was about to end, 'but do whatever you think is best.'

He was dressed for the practice in a smart dark suit and crisply laundered shirt—compliments of Hetty—and as the sheer masculine appeal of him made her blood heat she wished for a crazy moment that they could spend the day together. That they could forget the sick and ailing of the parish and drive into the countryside. Maybe have lunch at a wayside pub and stroll beside a lazy river.

Unaware of her imaginings, he was telling her, 'I *am* doing what's best. Hannah and I could get too used to being here with you and the boys. It's best that we go back home and get into the old routine again before I forget what it was.'

She flinched. It was gratifying to know that he'd appreciated being part of her family, but there was a down side to what he'd just said. There'd been a finality about it, as if the thought of doing something about making the arrangements more permanent had never crossed his mind.

But he *was* full of surprises and sometimes it *was* as if he read her mind. As she turned away to hide her disappointment he said casually, 'Don't forget that we've promised ourselves a day at the coast. We've got that to look forward to.'

Caroline eyed him dubiously. It had been her idea and it had lost none of its appeal, but it would be another instance of them being in his company, she and her sons getting closer to him, and for what?

He sensed her hesitation and wanted to know what was wrong. 'Have you seen enough of us this week?'

'No!' she protested. 'It's not that. I just don't want the boys to get too fond of you. If you suddenly disappeared out of their lives it would be hard for them to adjust, after spending so much time with you.'

'I see. So you think that we might have a role reversal— that *I've* become the "here today, gone tomorrow" person?'

She sighed. 'You know what I mean, Marcus, and, please, don't keep harping about what happened long ago. We're two different people now. Can't you let the past *be* the past? It's old history.'

'Yes, but, as we both know, history has a habit of repeating itself,' he said in a low voice, as if he expected an interruption at any second.

'In what way?' she breathed.

He took a step towards her and then another until their breaths were mingling, their eye contact mesmerising, and then, without answering her question, he placed his lips on hers and his arms went around her.

The clean, masculine smell of him was like heady wine. The sensation of their bodies meeting in the sudden frantic embrace was like a current being switched on, and as she responded to the need in him Caroline was praying that this was the second chance that she'd longed for...

From what seemed like a long way off she could hear Hannah and the boys in the garden, and as she and Marcus clung together, mouth to mouth, hard chest to quickening breasts and thigh to thigh, Caroline was aware that the voices were coming nearer. Any moment they'd be outside the French windows and this elusive, precious thing with Marcus would be out in the open.

He'd heard them, too, and he put her away from him

with a sigh. 'Duty calls!' he said with a tight smile. 'In the form of our children, the Cathedral Practice, the local police force and—'

'Uncle Tom Cobbley and all?' she said with a breathless laugh as she tucked in the cream silk blouse that went with her green suit. 'But tell me first, Marcus, before all these things bear down on us, were you referring to the spontaneous combustion that just sprang up between us or something else when you mentioned history repeating itself? I need to know.'

'The remark had various connotations,' he said as the rapport between them drained away like water down a plughole. 'You attract me sexually. You always did. The chemistry will always be there between us. But there has to be more to a relationship than just sex.'

'How very patronising of you to point that out!' she snapped, but he ignored her and went on coolly, 'I'm aware that John Lennox is part of your life and from what I saw in the surgery the other day it seemed as if you and he were extremely matey.'

'Oh! For God's sake!' she exclaimed angrily. 'You think that I'm going to run off with him, like I did with Jamie? But in the meantime you don't mind letting body take over from brain when the mood takes you. You have some nerve, Marcus!'

'*Are* we going to school today, Mummy?' Luke's voice said from the open windows. She eyed him blankly for a second and then, pulling herself together, managed a smile.

'Yes, of course you are. Say goodbye to Hannah and we'll be off.'

Without another glance at Marcus, who was standing motionless beside her, she picked up her doctor's bag and pointed the twins towards the car.

Ever since becoming a GP, Caroline had always made herself put personal problems to one side the moment she entered the practice, and today it was her intention that the self-imposed discipline should still apply. Her function was to treat the sick, and to do that efficiently a clear head and an uncluttered mind were essential.

But she'd reckoned without Marcus appearing in her consulting room within seconds of her arrival. Without giving her time to get her breath, he informed her, 'Social Services have been on about the child that you saw at the end of afternoon surgery yesterday.'

She frowned, peeved that he was on the job before she'd had time to take her coat off.

'And?'

'They say that they're going to check it out but the child isn't on their at-risk register.'

'So?'

'Well, were you sure that the ulcerated sore *was* a cigarette burn?'

'No, of course I wasn't,' she said quietly, hurt that he was questioning her professional judgement on the heels of the earlier vote of no confidence regarding her personal life. 'It looked like it. He was a dirty little urchin and the mother looked as if she could do with sprucing up, too. One often gets child abuse occurring in those circumstances.'

'It happens just as frequently in better-class homes,' he pointed out with calm reason. 'Stress comes from high living just as much as with those who reside in squalor.'

'Yes, well, thanks for the lecture,' she said frostily. 'Now, if you don't mind, I'd like to get on with my morning surgery.'

'Did you not think it might be impetigo?' he persisted.

She stared at him. 'Yes, I did. When you see his notes you'll discover that I've arranged for him to be seen at a dermatological clinic today.

'I rang Social Services on two points. One, because of the nasty sore and, two, because he was covered in bruises.

'I know that there could be perfectly good reasons for both conditions, but I had to be sure that they were made aware of what was going on. If the skin tests show impetigo I'll be relieved, but there has to be a reason for the bruises, too.'

'Point taken. No need to get fractious,' he said with continuing easiness as he prepared to take his leave. 'I was only too happy to ask your advice with regard to the poisoning case and thought that you might be interested in another point of view regarding this matter.'

'I am,' Caroline protested with rising colour, 'but just for once I'd like a vote of confidence, instead of the continual putting down that I'm subjected to.'

His face straightened. 'I've seen too many families brought to the notice of Social Services when there was no need,' he said tightly, 'and once they're in the clutches of that organisation, be there cause for alarm or not, the life of the family is never the same.'

Caroline felt her annoyance recede. He was right. In a similar case to the one they were discussing, she'd had a distraught mother from a caring, well-ordered home begging her to convince Social Services that the round, scabby mark on her son's leg wasn't a cigarette burn and that it had been caused by one of the screws of his skateboard breaking the skin when he'd had a fall.

The teacher at school had seen the mark and had notified the authorities, and the horrified parents had been questioned at length about the matter. They'd eventually convinced those investigating the injury that there had been no ill-treatment involved, but their confidence had been so badly dented that they'd been afraid to use any sort of discipline from that time on.

'You're right, of course,' she agreed in a milder tone, 'but what about the children who *do* need protection and don't get it because of the likes of us? Or because the hospitals and schools aren't vigilant enough? We owe it to them to report it if there's the slightest shadow of doubt about any injury or other condition that manifests itself. Don't you agree?'

'Yes, of course I do, but child abuse is a minefield for all concerned—the victim, the medical profession and for Social Services.'

'So what are we arguing about, then, if we're in agreement?' she asked with a wary smile. 'Or is it that our differences are so many that disagreement is a way of life for us?'

'We haven't had any disagreements during the last few days that we've spent under the same roof,' he pointed out, still in tones of sweet reason, 'but better to have the fires of disagreement in our veins than no fire at all.' On that note he left her, thinking bemusedly that the pearls of wisdom he'd just cast before her should have been of her scattering.

Her elderly female patient with the polymyalgia rheumatica was amongst her patients in the afternoon surgery. She'd come seeking a further prescription for the steroids that had been prescribed for the complaint, and while she was there Caroline suggested that she come in for a flu injection at the commencement of the winter.

The woman eyed her doubtfully. 'We're still in the middle of summer,' she protested. 'Do I have to decide now?'

'No, of course not,' Caroline told her patiently. 'October will be early enough. I'm merely making you aware that it would be a sensible precaution. Being on steroids, it could make you more vulnerable to infection.

'Make an appointment with the nurse when the time comes and she'll also give you an injection against pneumonia which will last for the rest of your life, unlike the flu jab which is a yearly precaution.'

The reluctant steroid-taker was followed by a mother with a nine-year-old boy who'd had a chesty cough for some weeks and was showing no signs of throwing it off. Caroline had already prescribed antibiotics for the child but he was still wheezing. After examining him once more, she told the concerned mother that it was possible the child might be suffering from mild asthma.

'He's got a new teacher,' the woman said, 'and he seems to be in continual trouble with her. Do you think it's stress-related?'

'It's possible,' Caroline agreed, 'although intrinsic asthma often follows a respiratory infection. I'm going to prescribe an inhaler and we'll see how he gets on with that.'

The young patient's bottom lip jutted mutinously at the idea, but his eleven-year-old sister, who had attended with them, murmured enviously. 'Cool!' And the moment of reluctance on her brother's part passed as Caroline and their concerned parent tried to keep a straight face.

'Can't Hannah stay a bit longer?' Luke pleaded that evening, as Marcus gathered their belongings together.

'Want to stay,' the little girl said tearfully.

'We don't want them to go,' Liam said, backing up the other two.

Caroline sighed. Neither did she, but it wasn't for her to voice the thought. If she did, Marcus might realise the true extent of her feelings for him, which wouldn't have bothered her one bit if the relationship between them had been what she wanted it to be. But she was a long way from feeling secure in his regard, and the fact that he seemed happier in Stephanie's company than her own didn't help matters.

Yet she couldn't help but make a plea of her own, asking Marcus, 'Will your aunt be well enough to look after Hannah if you're called out by the police tomorrow? You did say that Saturday night is when it all comes alive.'

'It is,' he affirmed, 'but Aunt Min doesn't seem to have suffered any ill-effects from the tests, and she's insisting that I don't rearrange my rota with the police.'

He frowned. 'All of which brings to mind once more the thought of how much her life is embroiled with ours.'

'Yes, but it's plain to see that she loves Hannah dearly,' Caroline protested, wondering what was coming next.

She did well to wonder.

'Yes, I know that, but if I'm going to stay in the area there are some things that I have to change.'

'What?' she gasped. 'You said when we met up again that you wanted Hannah's roots to be in this place. That was why you'd come back!'

'Yes, I did, and it *was* the reason…partly.'

'And yet you'd consider moving her again? It's not fair on the child. She needs a stable home life, not being shunted around from pillar to post.'

'Yes, well, that isn't the easiest thing in the world to provide when one is a single parent.'

'I've done it! So why can't you?' she ranted, now thoroughly rattled at the thought of him going out of her life again. 'If you're concerned about the demands you make on your aunt, you should get married again!'

'Are you volunteering?' he asked with steely calm.

Her anger was wiped out by sheer amazement. Had she heard aright?

'Why? Are you asking?'

'I might be.'

Her legs began to wilt beneath her and Caroline sank onto the nearest chair. In past moments of madness she'd allowed herself to dream of this moment, but there'd always been a very different scenario to the occasion—not the take-it-or-leave-it sort of proposal that was being thrown at her like a bone to a dog.

'You'd use me to further your own ends!' she hissed.

He winced and she watched the dark colour rise up his neck. 'We'd both have something to bring to the marriage. Liam and Luke would gain a father and Hannah a mother— *and* a proper home life into the bargain.'

'I don't believe I'm hearing this!' she croaked.

The word 'love' wasn't coming into it. Not even affection! It was a business arrangement he was suggesting and there'd be nothing in it for her. For her children maybe, for his daughter and for Marcus himself, as he'd been at pains to point out how much family life meant to him, but the focal point of any family were the parents and their love for each other, and that would be missing—on his part, anyway.

'Think about it,' he said casually, and if she hadn't seen how tightly he was gripping the handle of his suitcase she might have thought he saw it as of no more importance than discussing what to have for lunch.

He hadn't finished. 'And in the meantime I won't do anything until I have your answer.' On that note he went to stow his belongings in the boot of the car.

He could have it now, she thought raggedly. It was *no*! She'd had one go at a marriage without love and wasn't in the market for a second. How dared he ask such a thing of her! He was making her feel cheap and malleable, as if she were clay that he could mould in whatever way he wished.

Hetty and the boys came out at that moment to wave goodbye, and as Marcus began strapping Hannah into her car seat it was hardly the moment to shriek at him that he could take his marriage proposal and stick it somewhere! But when next they met he'd know. That was as certain as night following day.

As Marcus left his car on the forecourt of the central police station he could feel the throb of excitement that was always present in the city centre on Saturday nights.

The blare of loud music from the bars and cafés. Cinemas spilling forth audiences in the direction of late night buses or towards the take-aways, and the queues outside the clubs where doormen looked the would-be revellers over with hard eyes.

It was 'Saturday night fever' and he'd been called out to assist those who were about to discover that it had some unpleasant side-effects.

In this instance he was there to examine a member of the public who'd been brought into the custody office for damaging a shopfront on the main street.

The man had been extremely violent when arrested and had sustained some cuts and bruises. Having been seen by the duty sergeant, he'd been placed in a holding room until the police surgeon could examine him to decide if he was in a fit state to be detained and subsequently interviewed.

There was a Perspex observation window in the room, and as Marcus watched him from the outside the gaunt, bespectacled culprit suddenly flung himself across the intervening space and started beating at the window with his fists.

'Spent the afternoon in Yate's Wine Lodge,' the sergeant said laconically, 'after the shop in question had refused to give him his money back on a dodgy purchase.'

Marcus was eyeing the man in concern. Violent or not, it was his responsibility to make sure that the prisoner came to no physical or mental harm while in police custody.

Those brought into the police station under the influence of drink or drugs were often in no state to defend themselves. They were alone against the forces of law and order.

No matter what offence they might be about to be charged with, in the case of injury, mental problems, drunkenness and so on he was there for their protection.

He had the greatest respect and admiration for the way that the police force carried out their duties, but his responsibility was to the member of the public who found themselves on the wrong side of the constabulary for whatever reason, and now, as on many other occasions, there was a man who was drunkenly taking out his rage at life in general just a few feet away.

'I'm a doctor,' he told him carefully, dodging his flailing

arms as two young constables tried to restrain him. 'I'm
here to examine you.'

The sight of a body not in uniform brought the man to
a bleary standstill and he muttered, 'Don't need a doctor.
Want my money back.'

'He's well over the limit,' Marcus told them. 'I'll attend
to his cuts and then you'd better let him sleep it off, but
keep an eye on him. We don't want him choking on his
own vomit.'

The younger of the two constables was eyeing the culprit
sympathetically, 'Poor devil. He lives not far from me. His
wife's got multiple sclerosis. She's in a wheelchair. He
does everything for her.

'When we brought the shop manager out to look at the
damage he said that the fellow had bought a toaster off him
and wanted his money back because it didn't work, but he'd
refused. Said it had been dropped, and Harry here went
berserk.'

Marcus frowned. There was a stress factor here and a
sick woman, possibly already unattended for some hours if
her husband had spent the afternoon drinking. If what the
constable had said was correct, her circumstances would
have to be looked into. She couldn't be left alone overnight.
Social Services would have to be informed.

That was just the beginning. As the night went on and
the 'fever' reached its peak, Marcus was kept fully occupied as the police vans spilled out the rough, the wicked
and the over-exuberant directly into the custody area to be
sorted out.

The work was challenging. It made the adrenalin flow,
but whenever he had a moment's respite he sent up grateful
thanks for the two households that held his heart, where
precious children slept safely, watched over by women who
loved them, and in gratitude for that he was prepared to set
aside his own yearnings.

*   *   *

The phone rang late on Saturday evening and when Caroline answered it Minette Townsend's voice came over the line.

'I'm ringing to say how much I appreciate you looking after Hannah while I've been in hospital, Dr Croft,' she said warmly. 'It took away all the tension that I would normally have felt at leaving her. Marcus is a wonderful father, but he's also a very busy man and I do like to help him all I can. However, in this instance I wasn't able to do so and your assistance was much appreciated by all of us.'

Caroline smiled into the receiver. She liked this pleasant, kindly woman who, from the sound of it, had put her own life on hold to help her nephew and his small daughter, and in that moment she understood why Marcus might feel that it was time that his aunt was set free from the domestic shackles of his life.

But with that understanding was the knowledge that his suggestion that they marry could have come from the same line of reasoning—that as his wife she, Caroline, would leave Aunt Min free to have a life of her own.

Would he really do that, though? Ask her to marry him for so unloving a reason? She wished she knew.

'It was my pleasure,' she told the other woman as she gathered together her scattered thoughts. 'My boys loved having Hannah around, and Hetty, my housekeeper, made a great fuss of Marcus. My sister, who's staying with me at the moment, got on very well with him, too.'

'Ah, yes,' his aunt replied. 'That would be the blonde young lady that he gave a lift into the city centre just a few moments ago. She'd stopped by earlier, and when he was called out on police surgeon business she asked him to drop her off.'

Caroline's jaw dropped. Stephanie had been round at Marcus's house on his first night back home! What was she thinking of? Or maybe she'd been invited. Whatever the answer, she was going to have her hopes dashed when she found out that he had asked her older sister to marry him…and that she was going to accept.

It was just over twenty-four hours since Marcus had suggested they marry, and she'd been denied the opportunity of an angry refusal.

Since then she'd had time to think, and as she'd calmed down most of her thoughts had been centred on a kind of reasoning that asked what was wrong with second best if the real thing wasn't on offer.

Lots of marriages jogged along without being founded on a grand passion. How many times had she heard people say that friendship was a better base for wedded bliss than desire? But could they call themselves friends?

There was harmony between them when the children were there, but when they weren't she and Marcus seemed to alternate between peaks and valleys with disturbing regularity.

The desire was there, but it was a mad, rampant sort of thing that suddenly surfaced and just as quickly subsided.

Yet through all her confused reasoning one thought remained uppermost. If she wanted Marcus, she could have him. The opportunity to become part of his life was presenting itself. Even though there was little joy in the way the offer was being made, wouldn't marriage on his terms be better than no marriage at all?

Just as long as she could cope with the knowledge that he was using her to suit his own ends—that if he didn't have Hannah, a single mother with two sons and a poor track record where relationships were concerned wouldn't be his choice.

By six o'clock the next morning Caroline had already watched the sun rise, showered, had breakfast and was wandering aimlessly around the garden when the thoughts uppermost in her mind clarified themselves and propelled her towards the telephone.

She would never intrude on Marcus at home at this hour, but if there was a chance that he was still at the police station she was prepared to contact him there.

Now that she'd made her decision she couldn't wait to give him his answer. Maybe it was because if she left it any longer she wouldn't be able to go through with it.

'Yes, Dr Owen *is* still here,' the voice on the station switchboard told her when she'd explained who she was. 'It's been a very busy night, but I do believe he's expecting to have finished in about half an hour.'

Hetty came down as she was getting the car out, and Caroline asked her if she'd give the boys their breakfasts when they awoke.

Of Stephanie there was no sign, but that wasn't surprising. She rarely surfaced before lunchtime on a Sunday. In the middle of a restless night Caroline had heard her come in and had been tempted to go downstairs to challenge her about her secretive visit to Marcus's house, but had decided that her sister was a free agent. It wasn't for her to dictate what she did and where she went.

When Marcus came striding out of the police station Caroline was waiting, a slender figure in neat jeans and a white cotton shirt.

His dark attractiveness was blunted with weariness after a long night on police premises but it hadn't affected his powers of observation.

He saw her immediately, standing in the shadows of the building, and came across, his expression a mixture of surprise, and brief pleasure, followed quickly by alarm.

'What's wrong, Caroline?' he asked quickly. 'What are you doing here? Are the children all right?'

'Yes, yes,' she assured him with equal speed. 'Everything's fine.' And it was, now that they were together again, even though her appearance seemed to have thrown him into a state of shock.

'I was up early, and as it's such a lovely morning I thought I'd come to meet you.'

'How did you know that I was here?'

'Your aunt rang last night to thank me for having Hannah while she was in hospital and she told me that you'd been called out. It occurred to me that you might still be here and I rang up to check.'

She wanted to add that Minette had also told her that Stephanie had been visiting them but the words stuck in her throat.

If Marcus wanted her to know he'd tell her. In the meantime, why make herself out to be jealous of her own sister...even though she was?

He was smiling now that she'd convinced him there was no cause for alarm and her cheeks warmed as he said softly. 'After a night of attending the bad, the not so good and the downright ugly, you're a sight for sore eyes. There's an all-night café around the corner. Shall we have a coffee before we go our separate ways?'

'Yes, let's do that,' she agreed whimsically. She knew the place and it was anything but salubrious, with Formica-topped tables, spindly tubular chairs and coffee served in thick mugs to its clientele which was made up mostly of long-distance lorry drivers.

It was a far cry from a rose bower or a tranquil lakeside as a setting to tell Marcus that she was willing to accept his downbeat proposal, but perhaps it *was* the best sort of place to clinch the 'deal' that he'd suggested. He wouldn't be expecting anything spectacular amongst the overflowing ashtrays and stale, baked-bean leftovers.

'And so to what do I owe the honour?' he asked as they sipped lukewarm coffee.

Caroline flashed him a wary smile. 'It depends on what you're referring to—whether you mean me coming to meet you or the supreme gesture that I'm about to make.'

He became still and as their eyes met, the clatter of pots,

harsh voices and the grinding traffic on the street outside seemed to fade away.

Moments like this brought their own atmosphere, Caroline thought as their glances held. Emotions were all that mattered. The scent of roses meant nothing if the heart wasn't truly involved, and burnt toast could be the perfume of the gods if it was.

'What gesture is that?' he said at last.

'I've been giving a lot of thought to what you suggested with regard to our domestic arrangements,' she said soberly as realities came crowding in.

'And?' he breathed.

'As you pointed out so sensibly, the boys will benefit from a fatherly influence and Hannah needs a mother. So if you're willing to take the risk then so am I.'

For a crazy moment Caroline thought she saw amazed pleasure on his face, but it couldn't be, could it? Not with the sort of proposal he'd come up with. The suggestion had been made for one reason only—to make his domestic affairs less complicated.

Well, it might accomplish that, but the same effect wouldn't apply to her life. It had been running smoothly before he'd come back on the scene but now it was in chaos, and the chaos would increase if the wedding went ahead.

With Marcus permanently in her life, it would be just too complicated for words—and achingly unsatisfying. But, much against her better judgement, she'd just told him she was willing to give it a try, and now she was waiting to hear what he had to say.

It wasn't long in coming. 'You'll marry me?' he said, husky with surprise. 'On those terms?'

'Yes. I've just said so.'

'When?'

'As soon as you like,' she told him recklessly, with the feeling that she was treating what should be a joyous thing like a dose of medicine. The sooner it was swallowed, the sooner the taste went.

'I'll see that you don't regret it, Caroline,' he said in a low voice. 'Hannah and I will both be on our best behaviour.'

Caroline gave a sick smile. She didn't want them always on their best behaviour, especially not Marcus. She wanted him to take on the mantle of a normal caring husband and maybe, if he couldn't bring himself to love her as she wanted him to, at least they might find some level of happiness in the strange arrangement.

CHAPTER EIGHT

MARCUS reached across the table and took Caroline's hand. 'Let's go. We can't celebrate a future together in this crummy place.'

'So you think we have something to celebrate?' she asked wryly as he drew her to her feet.

'Don't you?'

Caroline sighed. 'I wish you wouldn't answer a question with a question.'

When they reached the pavement outside Marcus turned to face her.

'You have to be sure about this decision, Caroline,' he said carefully. '*I* think that it can only benefit all of us— you, me and most of all the children—but if you have any doubts, now is the time to come clean.'

She looked away. Of course she had doubts. Even a glowing bride to be would have them to some extent, but in her case they were multiplied a thousandfold because the word 'love' had never been mentioned.

Yet in this moment, when Marcus was offering her an escape, Caroline knew she wasn't going to change her mind. Uneasy now, in case he changed his, she reached up and kissed him swiftly on the cheek, saying lightly as she did so, 'I've said I'll marry you, haven't I?'

His response was swift and surprisingly urgent as his arms went round her and his mouth found hers. As her lips parted to receive the unexpected contact he murmured against them, 'When, then?'

If it had been ardour driving him, and not the desire to give Aunt Min her freedom or the wish to present the delightful Hannah with a new mother, his urge to tie the knot would have made her ecstatic. But the words of his proposal were burnt on her mind and so her reply to the question was in keeping with them.

'How about a month from today in the small nonconformist church beside the park that the children and I attend?' she suggested smoothly.

'I'd have liked it to have been in the cathedral as I love that place, but I know the Dean wouldn't marry us because I've been divorced whereas the Reverend Jefferson at my church might not be so rigid.

'I want Stephanie and Hannah to be my bridesmaids and the boys as pages. Does that meet with your approval?'

It would be too bad if it didn't as now she'd got the bit between her teeth. The thought of a wedding...her own...whatever the circumstances...was something to look forward to.

When she'd married Jamie it had been a pathetic hole-in-the-corner affair and there wasn't going to be a repeat, not to the outside observer anyway.

She knew her own worth now. She was an intelligent, classy woman, a good doctor and a loving mother to her adopted sons. It was time that she stopped feeling inadequate where Marcus was concerned.

'Er, yes, I suppose so,' he was agreeing, 'and what do I have to do regarding the event? Find myself a best man and hire a grey topper and tails?'

'Yes,' she told him calmly. 'If the marriage isn't going to be one of those made in heaven, at least we can make it a memorable ceremony.'

As he fixed her with thoughtful dark eyes she presented him with one more pronouncement to digest.

'And if, as I suspect, my young sister has yearnings towards you that you're not prepared to diminish, we either call the whole thing off or you let her down lightly. I care a lot for Stephanie and don't want to see her hurt.'

'I think we can count on it that your sister's desire for

my company will disappear when she hears that you're going to marry me, but either way I'll bear the second part of your ultimatum in mind,' he said slowly.

Were they really discussing one of the most momentous occasions in a person's life? Caroline thought raggedly. Anyone listening wouldn't have thought so.

But, she reminded herself, Marcus had been up all night, administering to the criminal fraternity and suchlike. The least she could do was bring to a close this discussion which had started on a moderately high note and was now rapidly veering downwards.

'You're tired,' she commented. 'It was thoughtless of me to foist my decision on you at this hour after the night you've had.'

'But you felt if you waited any longer you might change your mind?' he questioned with dry perception.

Caroline managed a laugh. 'How well you read my thoughts...and then perhaps, on the other hand, how little you understand me.'

She reached up and touched his cheek gently. 'Go home to Hannah and Aunt Min, Marcus...and get some sleep. We can talk another time.' He nodded in weary agreement and they made their way to their separate cars.

Desperate to witness the reaction of someone other than Marcus and herself to their marriage plans, Caroline cornered Hetty the moment she got back to the house.

The boys were still asleep, having been allowed to stay up late the previous night, and Hetty herself, in a sensible plaid dressing-gown, had just finished her breakfast.

'Marcus has asked me to marry him,' Caroline told her without preamble.

Hetty goggled at her in delighted amazement and Caroline thought edgily that her housekeeper's pleasure would be short-lived if she knew the reason.

But unaware that the announcement wasn't quite the cause for rejoicing that it might have been, Hetty chuckled gleefully. 'I knew it! From the moment I saw Dr Owen I felt he was going to be special. I can tell from the way he looks at you.'

Like an insect under a microscope, Caroline thought wryly, or a patient with a past history of unreliability.

'His eyes follow you around the room as if he's afraid to let you out of his sight,' Hetty was continuing with the same delighted enthusiasm, and Caroline wondered what she'd say if she told her that was because he didn't trust her.

'Do the children know?' Hetty asked.

'No, not yet. I've only just given him my answer.'

'I hope it was yes.'

She nodded. 'Mmm. It was yes.'

The beam on Hetty's face became even brighter. 'There'll be no cause to have any worries about their re-action,' she prophesied. 'He's just what they need.'

He's just what *I* need, too, Caroline thought, but am I what *he* needs, other than as a provider of domestic harmony?

And would Hetty be as happy about the arrangement when it became clear that they weren't sleeping together, as that was a situation she wouldn't be able to keep under wraps for long?

When Hetty had taken herself off to church and Luke and Liam slept on, Caroline wandered from room to room, trying to visualise what life would be like as Marcus's wife rather than his temporary hostess, and the more she thought about it the more she realised that she didn't want them to live in this house.

For one thing, it might be big enough for her present requirements but with Marcus and Hannah added to the household it would feel cramped, and if there was one thing she was going to need in this bizarre marriage it was space.

But the main reason was that she wanted them to start

even, not in her house or his—which was no bigger than hers—but in a home that they'd bought together.

She was smiling as she thought that tomorrow she'd tell him so. She'd already given him cause for thought with the wedding arrangements that she'd trotted out on the spur of the moment.

Now he was going to find that there was more to come, and why not? If he'd been anticipating a quick tying of the knot and then they'd sink into dull domesticity, he had another think coming.

There was a great deal of surprise and interest as the news of the impending nuptials of two of the partners spread around the practice, and in one instance a touch of sour grapes was evident.

Caroline heard Heather, the practice nurse, comment to one of the receptionists that Marcus Owen must be a glutton for punishment if he was willing to take on somebody else's brood, as well as coping with his own offspring.

As Caroline listened to what wasn't for her ears there was hurt inside her because the other woman couldn't be expected to know that the giving wouldn't be all one-sided—that she'd be bringing something to the marriage that far outweighed anything Marcus had to offer. Because she loved him.

When the disgruntled nurse went on to say that some women had all the luck, Caroline was sorely tempted to tell her that it was never wise to judge on outward appearances, but pride and the determination that nobody was going to find out that they were entering into a marriage of convenience had made her keep silent.

One of the reasons why news of the wedding was soon common knowledge at the practice was because, surprisingly, Marcus asked Geoffrey to be his best man, and with the purring condescension that was so much a part of their senior colleague, he accepted and then promptly told every-one about their plans.

'Why Geoffrey of all people?' she asked in mild protest when she found out.

Marcus shrugged. 'Well, I have no family. All my friends are abroad, and for all his airs and graces I don't think that the old fellow has much fun so I thought—'

'That you'd do him the honour?'

He smiled and, observing his expression in its softer lines, she wanted to reach out and touch the face that was never out of her mind. She wanted to caress the strong planes of it, the mesmeric mouth, and run her fingers gently around the eyes that seemed to read her every thought—except the one that mattered. But she'd taken the initiative twice before and where had it got her? Nowhere!

'You don't mind, do you?' he was asking.

Caroline brought her thoughts back into line with an ef-fort. 'What?'

He sighed. 'Me, asking Geoffrey to be my best man.'

'No, of course not,' she replied, and began to laugh.

'What's the joke?'

'We're going from one extreme to the other. A tiny bridesmaid and pages and a geriatric best man…and that's not the only thing that's amusing.'

'Oh?'

'Yes, there are those who think that you're a glutton for punishment, taking on a woman with a family, and in the same quarter I'm deemed to be lucky to have ensnared you.'

He frowned. 'And that's funny?'

There was no mirth in her now, just the urge to strike out—to make him understand that *she* didn't see it that way. That *she* was the one who was going to be punished in a marriage where the scales would be heavily weighted against her.

'No. It's not funny at all,' she admitted, and went to attend to her patients.

Ellen Walters was the first one to come through the door of her consulting room on that particular morning, and as the old woman stomped in, leaning heavily on her stick, Caroline wished that her first consultation of the day might have been with someone made in a lighter mould.

The old woman had a talent for homing in on every bit of gossip in the neighbourhood and usually had plenty to say about the transgressions of others, expounding morality as if she had a divine right. As she planted herself in the chair opposite, Caroline was quick to get in the first word.

'Good morning, Mrs Walters,' she said briskly. 'What can I do for you today? Is the gall bladder behaving itself?'

The elderly woman had previously had surgery on that part of her anatomy and, although she'd be the last to admit it, the operation, done by traditional methods, had on the face of it been a lot more successful than that of Minette Townsend's.

'It's better than it was,' she said grumpily, 'but it's not that I've come about. I need a repeat prescription for my arthritis tablets.'

'They would have given you that at Reception.'

She bridled. 'Are you saying that I'm wasting your time?'

'No, I'm not,' Caroline told her patiently, 'but if you'd asked the receptionist it would have saved yours—unless there's something else you need to see me about.'

It became obvious that there was, and it wasn't a medical matter. 'So you've let him put you in the family way?' she said.

Caroline stared at her. 'I beg your pardon?'

'I believe you're marrying that Dr Owen because he's put you in the family way.'

Outrage fought with amusement as she replied coolly, 'Yes, I am marrying Dr Owen and, yes, he is putting me in the family way, but I am not pregnant by him. Perhaps you could relay that fact to your source of information. The family that you've heard about is a ready-made one in the form of a tiny girl who'll be stepsister to my own children.'

The old woman didn't bat an eyelid. 'I see. Well, I'm glad to hear it. If you doctors can't set the rest of us an example it would be a poor state of affairs.'

Caroline went across to the door and held it open. 'Good morning, Mrs Walters. I hope that the gall bladder won't give you any more trouble.' As the local gossip got to her feet and walked slowly towards her she added, 'But I know that I can rely on you to let me know if it does.'

'Yes, you can,' Ellen assured her balefully as she departed.

Seconds after the door closed behind her it opened again to admit Marcus. When he saw Caroline's expression he asked, 'What's wrong? You look as if you don't know whether to laugh or cry. Has the old lady been ruffling your feathers?'

'That one has some gall!' she exclaimed. 'It's small wonder that she's suffered from bile accumulation.'

He threw back his head and laughed. 'I can see that she's really got under your skin.'

'Ellen Walters was under the impression that we were having to get married because you'd ''put me in the family way'' and was all set for giving me a talk on morals until I explained that nothing could be further from the truth.'

His face had darkened. 'You shouldn't have to account for yourself to a patient!' he growled.

'Correct,' she agreed with weary patience, 'but it would seem that our affairs are the main topic of interest at the moment, and as we're supposed to have known each other for so short a time I suppose that people are going to think that our marriage is a case of having to.'

He reached across and pulled her to him, and as her head nestled beneath his chin he said softly. 'But we haven't

only known each other for a short time, have we, Caroline?
We've known each other for ever.'

Yes! she wanted to cry, but not long enough to make
any babies together. Not long enough to be getting married
for the right reasons. And why did he have to start holding
her like this when they both had patients waiting to be
seen?

'Mmm. We have, haven't we?' she said flatly as she
moved out of his embrace. 'And if we don't get back to
work some of our patients will feel that they've been waiting for ever.'

'Yes, of course.' He was already making for the door
but had one parting shot to make. 'Don't take any notice
of what people say. It's what you and I think that matters.'

That was all very well, she decided as she reached for
the buzzer on her desk, but the trouble was that they
weren't thinking the same things.

Marcus called round with Hannah that evening, and when
Caroline opened the door to them the little girl laughed
delightedly and jumped into her arms.

As they eyed each other above her brown curls Caroline
felt a lump in her throat. It seemed as if Hannah loved her
already. What joy it would be if in time her father felt the
same.

Whatever the future held, at that moment she knew there
was a role for her in their lives, and the loveless wedding
she was contemplating didn't seem so empty after all.

The twins had heard Hannah's laughter and were on the
scene immediately to claim her. As the three children went
off to their own pursuits Caroline said, 'I'm glad you've
come. There is something I want to discuss.'

'You aren't the only one with something to say,' he said
with a quick glance at her face. 'I have news to impart.'

'You first, then,' she suggested, stepping back to let
him in.

'I've heard from the pathologist about our suspected poisoning.'

'Yes! And?'

'You were right, my clever, intelligent wife-to-be. It *was* aconitine poisoning. The other warring neighbour found that a bag containing the roots of the plant had gone from his garden while the big row had been in progress.

'He'd only recently realised how dangerous the plant is and had dug it out. The dead man, no doubt ignorant of its lethal factors, must have thought he was getting one over on his enemy, by taking what he mistook for horseradish. Then he ate some of it.'

'There must be a moral to that somewhere. The dangers of ill-gotten gains and the consequences thereof,' Caroline said with a shudder.

He nodded. 'And now it's your turn. What are you going to take the wind out of my sails with now?'

'I think we should buy a house jointly, instead of starting off our married life in either this house or yours.'

He was smiling. 'Is that all? I thought you were going to tell me that you'd decided to throw me over for Lennox, or that you'd never got a divorce from Durant, or at the very least that you'd decided to join some obscure cult.

'Of course we'll do that if it's what you want. I'd have suggested it myself but I didn't know how you'd feel about having to look for a new home. We can start house-hunting whenever you like.'

Caroline turned away. Everything was going too smoothly today—Hannah's delighted greeting, Marcus having no problems with moving house.

At that moment Liam fell off his bicycle, and as she dealt with his badly grazed arm it seemed that normality was back.

When it was time to take Hannah home to bed Marcus said casually. 'There was another reason for me calling round tonight.'

Caroline eyed him curiously. 'Yes?'

'I had an invitation to the Chief Constable's garden party and was asked to bring a friend along. I accepted, but had no idea who to take with me. I'd hesitated to ask *you* as, previous to our recent commitment, I hadn't exactly noticed you gasping for my company. But now that there's to be some permanency in our relationship, I thought maybe you'd come along.'

Caroline's heart skipped a beat in spite of the invitation being issued in such a stilted way. Why couldn't he have swung her off her feet and whirled her round in his arms, while pleading laughingly, 'Come with me, Caro.' It was what he'd have done once.

If he were asking anyone else he probably would act like that. She'd seen him teasing the staff at the surgery and joking with the patients. It was only her that he treated with such formality. She fancied him like mad but he couldn't see it.

However, occasions such as this rarely came her way, and if she was going to start as she meant to go on then socialising was part of the plan.

'I'd love to go with you,' she told him, her violet eyes beginning to sparkle at the thought. 'When is it?'

He hesitated. 'Saturday.'

'Saturday?' she cried. 'That isn't giving me much notice.'

Marcus looked away and she said flatly, 'Ah! I get it. You've asked everyone else and finally got round to me.'

He swivelled back to face her and there was nothing stilted about him now. 'Damn you, Caroline! Of course I haven't asked anybody else. Someone did drop a hint that they were free on that day, but it fell on stony ground. You're the obvious person to go with me. After all, we're supposed to be getting married, aren't we?'

'Was it Stephanie?'

'What? Who wanted to go with me? No. If you really

want to know, it was a patient. We got talking about it and she latched onto the idea of going with me.'

Caroline breathed a sigh of relief. Stephanie still had to be told that she was marrying Marcus and she, Caroline, had yet to find out just how deep her sister's interest was in him.

'So that's why you're inviting me,' she said, going back to the attack. 'To make the fact more believable.'

'Will you please stop holding an inquest on my motives?' he snorted angrily. 'You've said you'll go with me and now you're hedging.'

That was how it might appear, but she was going. Nothing would keep her away. The thought of dressing up to see some of the top brass of the police force in the Chief Constable's gardens, and eating afternoon tea with Marcus by her side in a huge marquee, was something she wasn't going to miss. It would be the first time they'd appeared in public as a couple and she needed something to boost her confidence.

'I'm not hedging,' she said in a softer tone. 'Merely trying to work out why you've asked me.'

He raised an ironic eyebrow. 'And have you come to a conclusion?'

'I think so.'

'And are you going to tell me what it is?'

There was laughter in her now, amusement at the crazy conversation they'd just had. It was clear that he'd left the invitation until the last minute because he'd expected her to refuse, but now that she was prepared to take the enormous step of marrying him, to ask her to go to the garden party must seem like a trifling request.

CHAPTER NINE

IN THE days before the event various things occurred, the first being a disconcerting confrontation later that night with Stephanie that left Caroline feeling edgy and unsettled.

'Marcus has asked me to marry him,' she said carefully when her sister arrived home after midnight.

In the middle of making herself a coffee, Stephanie became motionless. With the coffee-jar in one hand and a spoon in the other she said, without turning to face her sister, 'And as you're not in love with him, I take it you've said no.'

Caroline shook her head. 'As a matter of fact, I said yes.'

'You did?' Stephanie cried in amazement, and then with sudden censure, 'But how can you do that to him when you don't love him?'

'And I suppose *you* do,' Caroline said quietly.

Stephanie eyed her challengingly. 'You said that. I didn't!' There was denial in her voice, but when she gave up on the coffee and went straight up to bed she left behind an atmosphere of unspoken thoughts and desires that made Caroline wonder just what was going on in her sister's mind.

It was extremely busy at the practice during the rest of the week. Heather was on holiday and her temporary replacement was struggling to keep up with the workload. Added to that, Sue Bell was ill with a flu-type virus, and the absence of both women was being felt.

Having done his stint as police surgeon over the weekend, Marcus was free for the next fourteen days, for which both he and Caroline were truly thankful as they faced the seemingly never-ending throng in the waiting room.

Geoffrey was doing his share, but his late arrival on Mondays from his weekends away and his early departure on Fridays for the same reason left more for them to cope with.

As Caroline buzzed for her one remaining patient to present herself on the last day of the working week, she prayed that it wouldn't be anything too serious so that she could leave the demands of the practice with an easy mind for a couple of days. But when she saw the state of Noreen Gresham, she knew that it was a vain hope.

The fifty-year-old had suffered a brain haemorrhage some years previously which had left her with minor speech problems and some lack of movement in her left leg, and it was a deterioration of that same limb which had brought her reluctantly to the surgery.

A proud, independent woman, she was always loth to ask for help when health problems arose, as they often did, and when Caroline saw the distress she was in on this occasion she knew just how much it had cost the woman to make her way to the surgery.

'It's my leg, Doctor,' she said in a voice that was shrill with tension. 'The use has gone out of it. I'm having to drag it along.'

'Why didn't you send for me?' Caroline asked as she felt the coldness of the offending part and then helped Noreen off with her coat so that she could check her blood pressure. 'I've told you often enough that I'll always come out to you. How did you get here?'

'I came by taxi,' Noreen told her thickly. 'I couldn't manage the bus.'

Caroline sighed. 'I'm sure you couldn't in this state! Your blood pressure's sky-high in spite of the medication you're on and your pulse is racing. I know you're not going to like it, but I'm going to send for an ambulance to have you admitted to hospital for tests.'

The sick woman put out a hand as if to ward her off. 'No! I've seen enough of those places.'

'Yes, well, isn't it better to put up with just a little bit more to make you well again?' Caroline coaxed gently. 'Your family would be frantic if they knew you'd come here alone in such a state.'

As Noreen gazed morosely ahead, showing no signs of co-operating, Caroline decided that it needed shock tactics to convince her of the seriousness of her condition.

'It would appear that you've had a slight stroke,' she told her. 'Now do you understand why I want you in hospital?'

'I'd worked that out for meself,' Noreen choked.

'And so why didn't you get help sooner?' Caroline asked gently.

'I'm used to fending for meself. I don't want to have to be relying on others all the time.'

'Yes, I know,' Caroline sympathised, 'but sometimes we have no choice, Noreen. Now, shall I ring your daughter and ask her to meet you at the hospital?'

'I suppose so, but she'll go mad when she knows and I can't stand fussing.'

'Better that than if she didn't care about you,' Caroline pointed out as she picked up the phone.

The day of the garden party dawned wet and chilly. As Caroline surveyed the filmy dress of pale green silk and the wide-brimmed matching hat that she'd bought for the occasion, she thought ruefully that such finery wasn't going to be seen if she was going to be steaming inside a plastic raincoat.

She wanted to do Marcus credit in front of his associates in the police force and if she had to wear a mack or crouch beneath a big striped golf umbrella as they strolled around the sideshows and entertainments, it wasn't going to enhance her image.

But more than impressing the upholders of the law, she wanted her appearance to have an impact on her future husband. So far they'd never been in the same company socially. He was used to seeing her in the casual clothes she wore around the house or in the neat suits that were her choice for the practice—sensible attire that went with the image of the efficient Dr Croft.

Today, however, she had an insane urge to be neither sensible nor efficient...nor the caring mother figure. For once she was going to be frivolous and carefree, like a bird let out of its cage, and when the clouds disappeared at midday, to be replaced with the promise of a bright sunny afternoon, her spirits rose.

When the boys saw her in her finery Luke's eyes went to the hat. 'You look lovely, Mummy,' he said, 'like a pale green toadstool.'

She ruffled his hair gently. 'Thank you, dear. That's just the vote of confidence I needed.'

If she'd sensed any unease in her children when she'd told them she was to marry Marcus she'd have had grave doubts about the wisdom of it, but their delight had been plain to see. The whys and wherefores of it hadn't occurred to them. All they'd wanted to know was how soon and—thinking of their early morning cuddle—would he be sleeping in her bed?

To the first question she'd been able to answer, 'Yes, very soon.' The reply to the second had needed more finesse. 'We'll have to see how it works out,' she'd told them. 'Hannah may not want to be in a room of her own at first. Remember it will all be very different for her, becoming part of a new family...and moving to a new house.'

Both answers had seemed to satisfy them and after they'd gone back to their play Caroline had thought that it was going to be very different for all of them, but mostly for herself.

She'd be allowing the defences that she'd retreated behind over the years to be breached—not by pagan hordes or other marauding armies, but by a dark-haired predator of another kind, someone who from the moment of his return had invaded her peace of mind, her rigid self-control, and had made her long for the things that she'd previously decided were out of reach.

But today she was going to put all misgivings to one side and be a beautiful, entertaining companion to the man in her life, and when Marcus came to pick her up she went down the path to meet him with lightness in her step and a smiling challenge in her eyes.

His face was serious as he got out of the car, but his expression changed when he saw her. As if her mood was reaching out to him, he said with a husky laugh. 'You look very beautiful, Caroline. I'll have to keep my eye on the boys in blue or they'll be wanting to take you into custody.'

'Thank you,' she said with a mocking curtsey. 'That's the second compliment I've had. Luke thinks that I look like a green toadstool.'

He threw back his head and laughed, and she eyed him lovingly. There hadn't been much to laugh about in his life so far. He'd been let down by a fickle girlfriend long ago, lost a wife that he'd obviously cherished and now, as if he didn't want to give himself time to think, he was bringing up his daughter on his own, working as a GP and officiating as police surgeon.

In that moment she forgot her own unsatisfied longings and vowed that she and her family would bring joy into his life if he'd let them, that there would be more laughter and less heart-searching, and as she settled into the passenger seat the day seemed full of promise.

As they strolled in the gardens of the Chief Constable's

imposing residence Marcus took her hand in his and she
felt as if the sun was shining for them alone.

They were being given the chance to spend some time
together. Whether he'd planned it that way, or had asked
her to go with him because she was handy and available,
she didn't know.

What she *did* know was that there was no tension in
either of them today, and she vowed that nothing was going
to be allowed to change that.

Various people that he'd got to know in his capacity as
police surgeon stopped to chat, and as he introduced her as
his fiancée Caroline put the thought of just how much *that*
meant to the back of her mind and gave herself up to the
pleasure of being so described.

Those present appeared to be a mixture of the general
public, various local dignitaries, members of the council
and senior police officers and their wives, with a generous
smattering of the rank and file of the constabulary keeping
a watchful eye on the proceedings.

In fact, everywhere she looked there seemed to be a police constable standing nearby, and as they went into a huge
marquee for afternoon tea she asked curiously, 'Why all
the security, Marcus? It's making me feel nervous.'

'It's just standard procedure,' he said easily. 'There are
those who'd like to make a name for themselves by giving
the Chief Constable some grief, and if they succeeded it
wouldn't do much for the name of the force.'

'I don't suppose it would do much for him either,' she
commented drily.

'No, it wouldn't,' he agreed, 'but all of that isn't our
problem. We have enough concerns of our own to think
about.'

Her face straightened. 'I don't want to be reminded of
them, Marcus, not today.'

There was a marriage that she was entering into which
would be like walking on eggshells, and with it went the

trauma of stepping into another woman's shoes, plus a busy practice in which she played a vital role—and countless other drains on her time and resources that she didn't want to be reminded of just then.

'You'd rather live for the moment, would you?' he questioned, his dark glance unreadable.

She nodded mutely, knowing that if Marcus followed up the question with some sort of comment to the effect that it was nothing fresh, she'd want to go home.

He didn't. Instead, he took her hand and, raising her from her seat, looked down into her empty teacup. 'If you've finished, let's go. It's too hot and noisy in here.'

Caroline nodded. She wanted to be alone with him, not hemmed in with all these people, and for once it seemed as if their thoughts were running on the same track.

Maybe today it was all going to come right. The sky was blue and the scent of flowers was all around them, and for once they'd put their cares to one side. In a relaxed mood such as this, perhaps they could talk properly for once— clear the air and look forward to a new beginning.

It seemed that the feet of most of those present had been guided towards the food as when they left the tea tent the gardens were almost deserted.

Appreciating the unexpected tranquillity, they walked slowly over green slopes to where a gazebo stood, its graceful iron scrolls entwined with summer flowers.

Pointing to the seat inside, Marcus said, 'Shall we?'

She nodded, her heart beating faster. The magic was continuing. Was she crazy to let it go on?

The small iron bench wasn't very wide. Their thighs were touching and as Caroline felt the hard strength of him beside her the longing that his nearness always brought was there.

'Happy?' he asked quietly, turning towards her.

Their faces were almost touching. She could see the need for an answer to the question in his eyes. She was tantalisingly close to the firm mouth which had made her bones melt on previous occasions, and it would have been so easy to caress the dark waves curling above his ears.

But caution was reminding her that it had been she who'd taken the initiative on previous occasions, even though his responses had been immediate and passionate, and hadn't she vowed that the next time, if there ever was one, it would be Marcus who made the first move?

Yet, feeling as she did on this golden summer afternoon, there was no way she could deny him the truth.

'Yes, I'm happy, Marcus,' she told him, the brightness of her smile confirming the sincerity of her words, 'and if you want to know why, it's because for once we're at peace. We're in harmony, and I pray that we can stay that way.'

'Why shouldn't we?' he questioned carefully.

'Well, for one thing we're both wary, having had marriages that didn't last.' She turned her head away, swallowing hard. 'But although ours is going to be somewhat a union of convenience, I'm hoping that what we and the children contribute to it will be enough for us to find a degree of happiness.'

She'd felt him flinch while she'd been speaking, and when she faced him again it seemed as if some of the light had gone out of him.

'So you *do* have doubts?'

'Don't you?' she asked softly.

'Yes, I have my doubts,' he admitted, 'but I don't think they're the same as yours, and at this moment, with you sitting beside me looking totally relaxed, they seem a long way off.

'You say that your present happiness is because we're in harmony.' His voice deepened. 'And I'd hate to do anything to break the spell, but I'm going to risk it.'

Her eyes widened. What was that supposed to mean?

The answer was there as he reached out for her and took

her in his arms, and as they held each other in mutual need Caroline felt that maybe her prayers *were* going to be answered.

But delight only came in small doses, she thought ruefully as a child's voice, calling to an unseen parent, said from outside the gazebo, 'Mummy! There's a little house here, covered in flowers. Can we go in?'

'So much for the enchanted garden,' Marcus said with a wry smile as they drew apart.

The garden party was over and the guests were filtering homewards after a pleasant afternoon, Caroline and Marcus amongst them.

With his hand on the doorhandle of the car, he asked, 'Which way, Caroline? Shall we go home the quick route through the town or take the country detour?'

She smiled dreamily, contentment wrapped around her like a velvet cloak. 'The longest way, please, Marcus.'

'My thoughts exactly,' he said easily as he slid into the driver's seat.

There was a companiable silence between them as they drove home and she thought that this was how it should be. A man and woman in tune with each other.

As the car nosed its way through small villages set in a sweeping patchwork of fields she wasn't to know that a wrong note was about to be introduced into the idyllic afternoon. That harmony was about to be displaced by discord which wouldn't be of her making.

Turning into a narrow country lane which was barely wide enough for two vehicles to pass, Marcus had to brake sharply because the road ahead of them was blocked by a van and a big black car that just weren't going to get by each other.

That was the first thing that registered. The second was that the driver of the car, which was on the same side of the road as themselves, was shouting abuse, kicking the door and hammering furiously with his fists on the window of the van while the man inside cowered in the driver's seat.

'What have we here?' Marcus said grimly. 'Road rage?'

Caroline shifted uncomfortably in her seat. 'Turn back, Marcus,' she said quickly. 'We're not going to get through and the driver of the car is going absolutely berserk.'

His jaw had tightened. 'I can't just drive away. Whoever's to blame—and from the looks of it I imagine that neither of them were prepared to give way—the van driver's in danger of the other fellow doing him some serious harm.'

He gave a dry laugh. 'I *am* a police surgeon, and although I'm not on duty I can't stand by and let this sort of violence take place. The guy is going to murder him if someone doesn't intervene. I can see it coming.'

Even as he was speaking he was getting out of the car. Turning quickly, he instructed, 'Phone for the police on my mobile and, whatever you do, stay where you are and keep the doors locked.'

Caroline watched tensely as he went up to the attacker and tried to reason with him, but the man flung him to one side and ran round to the back of his car where he reached into the boot.

She could tell by Marcus's actions that while the car driver was gone he was trying to persuade the terrified van driver to join them in their vehicle until the police came, but he wasn't having much success.

They were parked behind the black car and she guessed that its driver wasn't aware of her presence as he grabbed a pickaxe out of the boot and began to move to where Marcus was trying to reassure the other man.

Marcus had his back to his assailant, and as she watched in horror a vision of the axe slicing into the man she loved propelled her out of the car.

The road-rager was moving swiftly but she was faster.

In three strides she'd caught up with him from behind. Flinging herself on him, she almost brought him to the ground, but weight was on his side and he threw her off, then swung round viciously with his weapon raised.

Her intervention had given Marcus time to realise what his intentions were and now it was his turn to attack from the rear and there were no doubts about it this time. As he grappled with the man the pickaxe fell to the ground and within seconds Marcus had him spreadeagled on the grass verge with the breath knocked out of him.

With his attacker now in a submissive role, the van driver ventured out of the cab, and as Marcus held the other man down he said urgently, 'Come and take over while I see to the lady.'

As the van driver obeyed him warily, Marcus ran over to where Caroline was sagging at the knees, her courage a thing of the past now that he was safe.

'Are you all right?' he asked hoarsely.

She nodded. 'Yes, but I've never been so afraid in my life!'

'That makes two of us,' he said grimly, but instead of holding her close in comforting reassurance he became still. As she eyed him questioningly the sound of sirens could be heard in the distance.

As the intrusive wail came nearer the man on the grass verge started to get up but the van driver, no longer in fear of his life, pushed him back roughly and planted a heavy boot on his chest.

Within seconds two police cars came roaring into the lane, only to come to an abrupt halt when they saw how it was blocked.

As she watched their crews spill out and come the rest of the way on foot, all Caroline could think of was that she needed Marcus to hold her close and then take her home—away from this awful incident which could so easily have harmed them.

But he was walking towards the policemen, his face tight and unsmiling. Accepting that the comfort she craved would have to wait, she went to their car and sank limply into the passenger seat.

However, she'd barely had time to settle herself before he appeared at the car window with a young policewoman beside him. As Caroline looked at him questioningly he said abruptly, 'I could be some time with the police so I've arranged for the officer to take you home in one of their cars.'

'I'd rather wait and go home with you,' she protested.

He shook his head. 'That isn't a good idea. Do as I say.' Addressing the policewoman, he said, 'See that Dr Croft has a cup of hot, sweet tea when she gets home, will you?'

Turning back to Caroline, he commented, 'The police will probably want to hear your version of the incident, too, but there's no need for you to hang around. If they do, they can interview you at home.'

In that moment all the emotions she'd experienced during the last half-hour were blotted out by anger. There had been the fear that the maniac with the pickaxe would harm Marcus, her terror when he'd turned his rage on her and then the exquisite relief when she'd found they were safe, but they were as nothing compared to the annoyance she was experiencing now.

What was the matter with him? she thought as tears threatened. He was treating her as if *she* were to blame for what had happened. Couldn't he see that at this moment, more than any other, she needed him with her for reassurance, instead of being bundled off home? Didn't he realise that if anything happened to him her life would be without purpose?

'You look pale! Are you all right? And where is Dr Owen?' Hetty asked when Caroline got back to the house, having insisted that the police car drop her off at the end of the road.

'He found himself involved in police affairs so I got a taxi and left him to follow on as I've got a headache.'

'Oh, dear! Maybe you should lie down for a while,' she suggested.

'Yes, I think I will,' Caroline agreed. It would be a chance to gather her confused thoughts together.

After she'd removed the green silk dress she drew the curtains in her bedroom and lay on top of the bed in her slip, gazing stonily up at the ceiling.

Was she being ridiculous, letting Marcus reduce her to this state? she asked herself.

No! She wasn't!

During the incident in the country lane she'd been really afraid. A normal reaction in the circumstances. The very thought of it made her mouth go dry, but there had been no way she could have stood by without doing something, and her intervention had saved Marcus from a vicious attack.

All right, she hadn't expected him to fall on her neck, weeping tears of gratitude, but neither had she expected the verbal frostiness which had been his reaction. Her hurt and anger hadn't abated when she heard swift footsteps coming up the stairs.

Raising herself to a sitting position, she waited for the knock on the door. When it came she called out coldly, 'Who is it?' As if she didn't know!

'It's me, of course,' he said. 'Can I come in?'

'Yes. Just as long as the fact that I'm only partly dressed won't be added to my other transgressions.'

He was beside her almost before she'd finished speaking, observing satin-smooth shoulders above the filmy slip that did little to conceal the springing nipples of her breasts and the promises of slender hips.

But he wasn't to be tempted. Caroline saw a pulse flicker below his jawline and there was a glint in his dark eyes, but it was brusque anxiety that came over as he said, 'So you're all right?'

'Yes, I'm all right,' she agreed grudgingly.

'But?'

'But I'm hopping mad at the way you bundled me out of the way.'

Marcus raised his eyes heavenwards. 'For goodness' sake! You almost got yourself killed on my behalf and that of the van driver. I nearly collapsed when I saw you clinging onto that maniac with the axe!'

'What was I supposed to do? Stand by and watch?'

'Yes,' he said through gritted teeth. 'You have two children dependent on you. Supposing you'd been killed. The state that fellow was in he would have seen the three of us off, given the chance.'

'You have a dependant of your own!' she pointed out coldly.

'Do you think I don't know that?' he growled. 'But the fact remains that I told you to stay put—and you didn't.'

'Yes, you did, but I don't remember agreeing to do so. I'm capable of making my own decisions. Heaven only knows, I've been doing it for long enough,' she snapped.

She'd wanted to get under his skin and she'd succeeded. With a hiss of anger he swooped down on her. Taking her by the forearms, he pulled her to her feet, and as they faced each other he said angrily, 'You'd be no good to either me or the children...dead.'

'That's it!' she cried, struggling to throw off his grip. 'The final insult! You're telling me that it would have been inconvenient if I'd died. I wouldn't have been there to fill the slot of stepmother-cum-hostess-cum-general factotum. Well, I've got news for you. The wedding is off!'

'Really?' he questioned silkily. 'I don't think so. I'm not going to allow you to go back on your word. You're going to marry me whether you like it or not.'

'Then maybe I would be better off dead,' she jibed.

His glance was on her smooth shoulders and the tangled chestnut hair and his grip tightened as he said softly, 'I'm sorry that you see marriage to me in that light, but think of your children. They're all for it. Why disappoint them because you're peeved with me? Why throw a tantrum like this?'

'Tantrum!' she shrieked, beating against his chest with her fists. 'You're the most insensitive man I've ever met!'

Marcus was smiling, but it didn't reach his eyes. 'If that's how you've got me labelled, I may as well play the part.'

With a sudden deft movement he slipped the straps off her shoulders. The satin slip fell to the ground and his lips went to the hollow between her breasts. The hands which had held her so tightly in anger became harbingers of passion as they wooed her senses.

In those incredible moments Caroline felt a whole range of emotions and among them was a heady sort of triumph because he *did* find her desirable—but was that it? Were they only to be compatible in lust…without love?

Did she want this frenetic coming together to lack the other feelings that made a good relationship? No, she didn't, and with a groan that came straight from the depths of her being she pushed him away.

His face became blank. 'What have I done now?'

'Nothing, Marcus, except to make me realise that I'm not in the lust-without-love market.'

'I see. So that's your excuse this time. I'm well aware that you always come up with a reason for removing yourself from my arms. You talk about lust without love. Are you sure that you aren't just a tease, Caroline? Leading me on and then backing out at the last moment?'

'You have some nerve!' she breathed.

'Yes, I have, haven't I?' He was moving towards the door and as a parting shot he said, 'If I hadn't, I might be thinking twice about what I'm letting myself in for. Oh, and with regard to our forthcoming nuptials, I'll pick you up tomorrow morning *en route* to the estate agents.'

On a centre page of the Sunday paper the headline read, POLICE SURGEON AND LOCAL GP INVOLVED IN ROAD RAGE INCIDENT.

'No wonder you had a headache!' Hetty exclaimed when she saw it. 'I understand now why Dr Owen was in such a state when he got here yesterday afternoon. He went up the stairs three at a time.'

During the long hours of a restless night Caroline had thought illogically that where his high-handed attitude regarding her participation in the incident had infuriated her, his insistence that she was going to marry him whether she liked it or not had been oddly comforting because the moment she'd told him that the wedding was off she'd regretted it.

And today, remembering his final comments, they were going house-hunting, and as they seemed to agree on very little the exercise would no doubt turn out to be just as traumatic as everything else in their lives.

Thinking back to the blighted golden promise of the previous day, there was sadness in her. The magic of those moments in the gazebo had been an enchanted extension of the contentment she'd felt from the moment she'd put on the beautiful dress and hat and gone forth to meet the man she loved.

But she'd reckoned without the actions of three men—two of them stubborn motorists, and the third? Too wrapped up in his own opinions?

CHAPTER TEN

THE turbulence of the previous day had given way to peace as the five of them viewed various dwellings in the area. Maybe it was the presence of the children that brought balance to the atmosphere, or perhaps Marcus had decided that least said, soonest mended with regard to their heated words and behaviour in her bedroom.

Whatever the reason, Caroline was grateful for the return to normality and when they compared notes, after viewing half a dozen properties, she was amazed to find that they were in agreement that a solid Victorian house with six bedrooms, a small orchard and a stream running through its gardens was the home for them.

It was near enough to the practice and yet far enough away for the two doctors to feel that they weren't living quite so much on top of the job as they were at present.

There was just one small blight on the unity of their thoughts as she did a quick calculation on the allocation of bedrooms and wondered if Marcus's mind was moving along the same lines as her own.

They'd need a room for Hetty, one for the boys, another for Hannah and a guest room. That left two, and the obvious conclusion that she and he would take one each.

But the house had a delightful master bedroom. Maybe he'd suggest that they toss a coin for it, and what if he did? She'd known from the beginning that was how it was going to be. Raising her eyes heavenwards, she wished that the departed Kirstie would send a sign that would show her the way to Marcus's heart.

'So? What do you think?' he asked as the estate agent hovered expectantly.

'I think that this is the place for us,' she said gravely. 'The children will love it here.'

'Yes, they will,' he agreed. 'But what about you?'

Her heart cried, 'Whither *thou* goest I will go.' But, having refused to marry him only hours earlier, she could imagine the reception that would get!

'If there *is* a right place for us, I think that this is it,' she told him, and saw him wince.

'So you have doubts?'

'Only about ourselves...not about the house.'

The estate agent, sensing a switch of interest, asked quickly, 'Do you have a property to sell?'

'Yes, we have two properties that need to go on the market,' Marcus told him, coming back to the present moment, 'and we need a quick sale on each of them.'

'Well, now's the time to do it,' they were told. 'The housing market is booming at the moment and if you'd like to come back to the office we can take down some details with regard to your sales and the purchase of this property.'

By the time they'd made an offer for the new house and arranged appointments for each of their own properties to be valued it was lunchtime, and as they drove in search of somewhere to eat Marcus said, 'You're very quiet. Not having regrets about the house already, are you?'

Caroline shook her head. 'No, of course not. It's lovely. I was just thinking how one's life can change so drastically in so short a time.'

'True,' he agreed. 'Both our lives have altered in recent weeks. You're assuring me that you've no regrets about the house we've chosen so am I to take it that your pensive manner is still connected with second thoughts about the marriage?'

He'd put the question with a sort of calm matter-of-factness, but there was an undertone in his voice that she couldn't make out. If it had been anybody else, she might have thought that it was anxiety, but after his flat refusal to let her call the wedding off and her falling in with his ultimatum so meekly, it didn't seem likely that he was worried on that score.

'No, of course it isn't. I admit that I'd be happier if we were getting married under other circumstances, but we're both mature adults with growing families and I can't deny that a pooling of our children and our resources is a good idea.'

'And that's it? A good idea?'

They were in the process of pulling onto the forecourt of a local restaurant and as he stopped the car they faced each other. 'Why? Do *you* see it as something else?' she challenged.

'Maybe.'

'Maybe!' she hooted. 'Well, I won't be holding my breath on that one, just as I won't be trying to force my feet into your dead wife's shoes.'

He was frowning. 'You're jumping to conclusions again, Caroline. I wish you wouldn't. But there's been enough talking for one morning. The children are hungry. Let's eat.'

On Monday morning the whole practice was agog over the events after Saturday's garden party, and Caroline and Marcus had to reluctantly accept that they'd achieved celebrity status overnight.

Recalling the flare-up they'd had because of it, she felt that it was the last thing she wanted to be reminded of, but in view of the interest it was generating there was little she could do but oblige with the details.

Sue was back after her recent illness, and later in the morning she asked, 'Are you having a white wedding?'

'No, I don't think so,' Caroline told the likeable young receptionist. 'We've both been married before and have ready-made families so I hardly feel that a bridal gown and veil are called for.'

'So what, then?' Sue wanted to know.

'I haven't decided yet, but I don't want anything too severe as I'm having two bridesmaids and the boys are to be pages. Would you like to come along to help me choose something next Saturday?'

'I'd love to,' she said, beaming her delight. 'It's not all that long since my own wedding. It'll bring back all the excitement!'

'Really? Well, that's fine, then,' Caroline said with the feeling that Sue might end up getting more pleasure out of the shopping spree than she did.

When surgery was over Marcus came into her room and out of the blue she asked the question uppermost in her mind.

'What was the virus that your wife died of?'

He stared at her. 'Whatever brought that to mind?'

'Our conversation yesterday, I suppose. I've wondered why she went back to nursing so soon when she had a young baby to care for. Was it because you needed the money?'

Marcus shook his head. 'No. It was for another reason...and the virus was never fully identified.'

His face had closed up, as if the subject wasn't an easy one to discuss, but he went on to say, 'I suppose she wasn't any different from you when you adopted the boys. You'd have wanted to carry on with your profession.'

Caroline shook her head. 'Yes, I did, but for the first three years of their lives I lived on my savings and what benefits I could claim. I didn't come back to health care until I felt that we'd bonded with each other. Liam and Luke had already lost their natural mother and I didn't want them to feel that their adoptive parent was never there.'

'Very commendable,' he said gravely. 'You never cease to amaze me. In Kirstie's case it was different. She couldn't wait to get back to her job. The previous year she'd been voted top nurse and it had gone to her head.

'From a quiet little thing she became a ruthless worka-holic, determined to get to the top. Hannah and I came a poor second best. So now you know the sort of act you have to follow. It shouldn't be hard.' Leaving Caroline staring after him, open-mouthed, he returned to his own sanctum.

Aghast at the revelation of his flawed marriage, she would have followed him, but Geoffrey appeared at that moment and there was no way she wanted him to tune into anything connected with their private lives.

When he called Marcus back in to join them she'd managed to get her GP's hat back on, and with a quick sideways glance at her future husband's set face she braced herself for whatever was to come from the senior partner.

It wasn't what she expected.

'I was wondering what you'd like for a wedding gift,' Geoffrey said as she seated herself behind her desk and Marcus perched on the corner of it. 'I hear that you're considering buying a Victorian residence and, knowing how cold and damp those places can be, one or two things have come to mind that I thought I'd bounce off you both to get your reaction. Yes?'

'Yes, of course, Geoffrey,' Caroline murmured uncomfortably, while Marcus gave a polite nod.

Taking a piece of paper out of his pocket, Geoffrey began to read from it, and as they listened it was all they could do to keep straight faces.

'I thought maybe a humidifier to control the dampness,' he said in his usual patronising manner, 'or a hostess trolley to keep the food warm against the chill of the rooms. Maybe antique stone hot-water bottles, uses self-explanatory, or some of the special socks that the Victorians used to cover the claw feet of the bath.'

He raised a bushy grey eyebrow. 'What do you think?'

Caroline couldn't trust herself to speak, without laughing openly, but Marcus found his voice. 'We'd have to give the matter some thought, if you don't mind, Geoffrey. It's quite clear that you're expecting a drastic drop in our living standards and maybe we haven't given the matter enough consideration.'

The older man inclined his head graciously and went on his way. Once the door had closed behind him they collapsed into mirth.

'I'm surprised he didn't suggest presenting us with a cat's whisker radio or a DIY dampcourse,' she gurgled.

'Or a set of antimacassars,' Marcus hooted. 'What *is* the guy on about?'

Caroline wiped her eyes. 'His flat upstairs is very modern and trendy, considering his age, and Geoffrey obviously thinks that anyone whose taste differs from his is beyond the pale.'

'And so what do we tell him?' Marcus asked, trying to remain serious.

'I suggest that we go for the hot-water bottles,' Caroline suggested. 'I've seen them in use where they made excellent doorstops.'

Geoffrey's bizarre wedding-gift suggestions had lifted the gloom left in the atmosphere after Marcus's bald description of his marriage, and where she might have hesitated to say anything further on an obviously painful topic, now, after these moments of shared laughter, it was easier to say carefully, 'I had no idea that your marriage was about as disastrous as mine. Are we fools to contemplate another possible catastrophe, Marcus?'

Her arms ached to hold him, to comfort him for long past hurts but she sensed that the question had raised old barriers again.

'Maybe,' he answered flatly. 'Only time can answer that. But, then, if I remember rightly, you were always ready to take a gamble.'

The afternoon spent shopping with Sue Bell was pleasant and satisfying. Caroline bought herself a calf-length dress of stiff ecru silk, low-cut at the front with long sleeves and a full skirt.

The colour and sheen of the fabric made her skin look like alabaster and her hair a glinting brown coronet, and when she stepped out of the cubicle in the dress Sue nodded approvingly.

'You look stunning!' she enthused. 'I hope that Marcus knows he's a very lucky man.'

Caroline swivelled to face her. It was the kind of run-of-the-mill remark that people made in this kind of situation, she thought, but was there something else behind it. Did Sue guess that the love was all on one side?

'Why? Do you think there's a chance that he might need reminding?' she said quietly.

Sue's face went scarlet. 'No, of course not. It's just that he's so amiable and relaxed when he's with the rest of us, but when you appear his mood always changes.'

'And not for the better, you're saying?'

'No, I didn't mean that,' she protested. 'It's as if you mesmerise him.'

'Me! Mesmerise Marcus Owen!' she said derisively, dangerously near to giving the game away. 'Not guilty. The man has a mind of his own and when it's made up nothing will change it.'

He'd labelled her as fickle all those years ago and so far she'd seen no signs of him changing his mind about that—unless the offer of a marriage of convenience was a sign that he had, but she didn't think so.

The conversation with Sue rankled and on impulse she began to try on lingerie, wisps of satin and lace and sheer nightgowns.

So Marcus was 'laughing boy' when he was with the female staff of the practice, was he? But not when she was around, which made them think that he wasn't as taken with her as one would have expected.

Maybe the other woman thought her a cold fish. That he deserved something better…like one of themselves. Well, Sue could go back and tell them that she wasn't intending to wear flannelette in bed or calico next to her skin during the day.

As the shop assistant folded the dress and the lingerie that she'd chosen, Caroline transferred her thoughts from Marcus to her attendants.

'Would it be possible to have two bridesmaids' dresses made up out of the same fabric but in a different colour?' she asked.

The assistant smiled. 'Yes, of course. We need a couple of weeks' notice, though. When is the wedding?'

'In two weeks' time.'

'Oh! That's cutting it fine, but bring them in as soon as you can and our seamstress will take their measurements.'

As they left the small, exclusive shop Caroline was tempted to tell Sue that the lingerie had been bought in bravado and that if Marcus ever saw it the only emotion present would be passion, but she refrained because she knew that if she were ever to put into words what was lacking in their relationship it would be admitting defeat.

Once the statement was made there would be no taking it back. If it got around the practice that their forthcoming marriage wasn't exactly a love match, the staff would know immediately why she didn't switch him on like the rest of them did.

But there had been times when she'd done just that…switched him on. Maybe it hadn't been for the right reasons but they'd ignited nevertheless. Like the day of the garden party in her bedroom when Marcus had slid the straps of her slip off her shoulders and they'd gone on from there—until she'd recovered her sanity.

With the wedding only two weeks off, Caroline wished she hadn't been so hasty in naming a date. Apart from the arrangements that had to be made, she was assailed with the feeling of being swept along in a fast current of her own making.

At the time a month had seemed an eternity to wait before marrying Marcus, but in saner moments she wondered why she'd felt the need to rush into a marriage that was more of a business arrangement than a love match.

The minister at her own small church, a kindly, grey-haired cleric, had eyed her keenly when she'd requested that he marry them, and then had told her that he'd be only too pleased to do so just as long as it was what she wanted.

'It's what I want,' she'd said with wry truthfulness. 'It's what I've always wanted, but now that the opportunity is here it isn't exactly how I'd imagined it would be.'

'Do you love Marcus Owen?' the minister had asked.

'Yes,' she'd replied simply.

'Then you have my blessing.'

They'd both found purchasers for their properties but it went without saying that it would be some time before they were able to move into their new home as even the speediest of solicitors wouldn't have all the ends neatly tied up by their wedding day.

As the practice was closed on Saturday afternoons it had been possible to invite all the staff to the service and a reception at a nearby hotel.

The only other guest, apart from their respective families, was John Lennox, who'd been in a state of amazement ever since Caroline had told him she was marrying Marcus.

'You hardly know the man!' he'd expostulated. 'What has he got that I haven't?'

She'd laughed, amused at his scandalised expression. 'The inclination to marry me.'

'And you think I haven't?' he'd asked.

'Yes. You're married to the job.'

He'd smiled, his good humour returning. 'Yes, I suppose I am, although of late my attention has wandered a couple

of times. Good luck to you both, Caroline. I hope that
you'll be very happy.'

'I intend to be,' she'd told him convincingly, and had
wished she'd been as sure of it as she'd sounded. 'And
Marcus and I haven't just met. We knew each other when
we were medical students.'

'And you each married somebody else?'

'Yes. In my case disastrously.'

'And in his?' he'd questioned curiously.

'She died.'

There had been no way that she'd have told John that
Marcus hadn't been all that happy either.

'Not in childbirth?'

'No, but shortly afterwards.'

When she'd thought about the conversation afterwards
Caroline had known that Marcus's first marriage hadn't
been the only thing she hadn't been frank about. John
would have thought her insane if she'd told him the truth
about their relationship.

There were other things, too, that had to be dealt with
besides wedding arrangements in the form of morning and
afternoon surgeries with a senior partner who was hinting
at retirement and had already commenced the slowing-
down process that preceded it.

Sometimes at the end of a busy day she might be forgiven for thinking that nothing had changed—until she
opened the wardrobe door and saw the cream silk dress
hanging there.

Her relationship with Marcus in those last two weeks
before the wedding was friendly but guarded. They discussed the children, the house they were buying together,
the sale of their own properties, the ceremony, the reception—everything under the sun except themselves.

If Caroline had found more time on her hands she might
have thought twice about what she was letting herself in
for, but instead she wrapped herself in the needs of her

sons and her patients and in that safe cocoon let the days go past.

When David Grice walked into her consulting room one day she recognised him as one of the parents she'd seen in the school playground when she'd dropped Liam and Luke off.

A pleasant, fair-haired man, he was one of the many caring fathers to be seen there, and as he seated himself across the desk from her she wondered what had brought him to the Cathedral Practice.

It transpired that he was suffering from insomnia and consequently was continually exhausted, a state of affairs that wasn't conducive to family harmony.

'What's your job?' she asked.

'I'm the manager of a hospital trust,' he said lethargically.

Caroline eyed him sympathetically. 'Say no more. Balancing the books here at the practice is bad enough, but when one is on your level of stress the health risks are phenomenal. Do you bring work home?'

'Yes, and I often need to stay late because of meetings that we haven't been able to fit in during the working day. All of which I could cope with if I was getting a good night's sleep...but I'm not. The moment my head hits the pillow I'm living the day all over again—the frustrations, the harassments and the rest of it. It's making me irritable and I'm taking it out on my wife and family. That why I'm here, Doctor. I need help.'

'Yes, you do,' she agreed. 'The stress of the job and the lack of sleep are taking their toll, but before I prescribe anything I'm going to take your blood pressure, listen to your heart, take some blood...and I'd like a urine sample.'

'What for?'

'To test your blood sugar.'

David Grice's heart and blood pressure showed no cause for alarm and his urine was free of excess sugar. The results of the blood tests, checking for anaemia and poor thyroid functioning among other things, would take ten days to come through, and in the meantime there was the subject of depression to discuss. It was an area of medicine that was a veritable minefield as the illness wasn't easy to pinpoint.

'Obviously we'll have to wait until the results of the blood test come through,' she told him, 'but I think that your problem is going to prove mental rather than physical—that you're suffering from depression brought on by overwork and stress. Do you have rapid mood swings?'

He thought for a moment. 'Yes, I suppose I do. One moment I'm on top of the world, the next I feel suicidal. I never used to be like that.'

Caroline nodded. 'I'm going to give you a month's supply of something that will help you to sleep, and in the meantime let's see what sort of results we get from the blood tests.'

She was smiling to take the sting out of her next observation. 'If you're so stressed jobwise, why not let your wife take your children to school each morning?'

'It's the only chance I get to see them,' he said with unconscious bitterness. 'They're in bed when I get home in the evening.'

'I'm told the trust that you manage is one of the best-run in the area,' she said encouragingly. 'It seems a shame that you should have to suffer for your own excellence, but from what you've told me you do need to slow down. Is it too much to suggest that you ask the directors for more financial help and extra staff?'

'I could do that, but as we work on a tight budget the chances are that my request won't get anywhere.'

'Well, in that case I suggest a long holiday. The schools break up at the end of the week. Have you anything planned?'

'A couple of weeks in Spain.'

'Take advantage of them, then, and see if you can tag another week on.'

He nodded sombrely. 'I love the job, you know. There's a lot of satisfaction in being able to give proper health care to the public, but at the moment I don't seem to be coping in any area of my life.'

Caroline eyed him thoughtfully. Many young husbands who were achievers in their careers had to battle against stress, and often their partners were so busy proving that they, too, could have a career that the main breadwinner of the family didn't get the support he needed.

'With regard to the tablets that I'm going to prescribe to help you sleep, you must only take one every other night,' she told him. 'I don't want a situation to develop where you become too reliant on them for a good night's rest.'

When David Grice had gone Caroline found herself taking stock of her own busy life. She had always coped with the demands of her job and revelled in her role as mother to Liam and Luke.

Would marriage to Marcus tip *her* over the edge because of pressure? Or would it, even in its less than rapturous state, bring happiness and contentment? She wished she knew.

As if he'd tuned in to her doubts and deliberations, the bridegroom-to-be appeared at that moment and asked briefly, 'Are you going home for lunch?'

'No. Have you forgotten that the bridesmaids are being measured for their dresses today? We have to be at the boutique at a quarter to one. Stephanie's picking up your aunt and Hannah and I'm meeting them there. Why do you ask?'

'I thought we could have a bite together and sort out one or two minor matters at the same time, but obviously the dresses come first.'

'Minor matters—such as?' she asked curiously.

'Are we intending to have a honeymoon?'

'And that's a minor matter?'

'It must be,' he replied drily, 'as you haven't brought the subject up so far.'

'It hasn't been discussed because of the circumstances that prevail,' she said coolly, as if the thought of honeymooning with him wasn't like paradise beckoning. 'We have three children between us and we couldn't ask Hetty and your aunt to cope with a trio of lively youngsters for twenty-four hours a day while we swan off into the wild blue yonder.'

He raised a dark eyebrow. 'So? That isn't a problem. We take them with us. It hadn't occurred to me to do anything else. But perhaps you're using them as an excuse because you don't fancy the two of us being in such close proximity for any length of time.'

'Now you're putting words into my mouth,' she said stonily.

'I'm right, though, aren't I?'

She wanted to yell at him, No, you're not. To be close to you is all I've ever wanted, but you've never said you love me and I'm not going to get down on my knees and beg. *That's* why I want to avoid any real intimacy between us.

Instead, she parried, 'And supposing we did go away…where would you suggest?'

'Canada. It's a beautiful country.'

'Where exactly?'

'Anywhere you like. Vancouver, Toronto, Quebec. I remember a beautiful little town not far from Niagara that was like something from *Gone With The Wind*, with just one main street of quaint shops that were filled with all kinds of delightful things.

'The houses were white with verandas, and they had the greenest lawns I'd ever seen. There was something clean and untouched about the place. I've never forgotten it.'

'You said "I",' she probed. 'Didn't you go there with Kirstie?'

He eyed her blankly for a moment. 'Er...no. She was otherwise engaged.'

'Doing what?'

'Like I told you...aiming for perfection.'

'All right,' she agreed. 'If that's what you want, we'll go there. We never did get that day at the coast, did we? Hannah might be a bit young for that kind of holiday, but I'm sure she'll be happy enough with us all there together.'

'I never expected you to agree,' he said slowly.

His eyes had brightened. The strong planes of his face had softened at her words. There was pleasure beyond description in the knowledge that she'd pleased him. When he leaned forward and pressed his lips to her brow the gesture, though passionless, was another thing to treasure.

'I'll go and sort out a hotel and book the flights the moment surgery is over, if that's all right with you,' he said promptly.

Caroline smiled. What had started off as a somewhat barbed discussion had ended in harmony.

'There are still some things that need finalising,' she reminded him.

'Such as?'

'Which house are we going to live in until the new purchase is completed, and then there's your aunt. What are her plans now that freedom is within her grasp?'

'Aunt Min doesn't want to be too far away from us. I believe she has her eye on a nearby retirement apartment, which would give her the best of both worlds, don't you think?'

'Yes, I do, and with regard to Hetty I'm delighted that she's willing to stay on as housekeeper—but let's talk about those sort of things away from the surgery. How about tonight? I could come round to your place once the boys are in bed. Eight-thirty?'

'That would be fine,' he said as Alison Spence, the practice manager, came to tell them that a pharmaceutical salesman was waiting to claim their attention.

For the rest of the day Caroline was in high spirits. A fortnight in Canada with Marcus and the children was a bonus she hadn't expected.

His suggestion, though taking her unawares, had caught at her imagination. Not just the sound of the idyllic place that had so impressed him on a previous occasion, but because they'd be away from the eyes of those who knew them during those first few days of adjustment.

Hopefully, by the time they got back she'd know the score, and if it didn't add up to what she wanted it to she'd have only herself to blame.

'The police are on the line for you, Marcus,' Aunt Min said that evening, shortly before Caroline was due to arrive.

He frowned. Surely they weren't calling him out. He'd done his stint the previous weekend, but it had been known for the police surgeon on call to be unavailable for some reason and in that event the forces of law and order contacted one of the others on the list.

However, the terse message that came from the other end wasn't to request his presence at the station. It was to issue a word of warning, and as Marcus replaced the receiver his face was set in tight lines.

As it was a warm, dry night, Caroline decided that, instead of driving to Marcus's house, she'd cycle there, taking a short cut through the park.

She supposed that it would have been simpler for him to come to her place, but she felt that while he'd seen an abundance of her domestic set-up she'd seen very little of his.

One of the surest ways to get to know someone was in their home surroundings, and as in the very near future his home surroundings would be the same as hers there was a need in her to familiarise herself with all aspects of his life before that time arrived.

As she cycled towards the lake, which was shimmering in the evening sunshine, Caroline saw a man gazing sombrely into its depths and she felt the stirrings of alarm as she recognised David Grice.

What was he doing here alone beside the lake? she wondered. It was only that day that she'd diagnosed him as suffering from depression, and if the look on his face was anything to go by he hadn't cheered up at all.

'Hallo, David,' she said easily as she dismounted. 'We meet again.'

'My wife says she's going to leave me,' he announced in a flat, lifeless voice, without taking his eyes off the water.

'And why is that?' Caroline asked.

'She says I'm impossible to live with.'

'Does she know that you aren't well?'

He shrugged. 'Maybe. Maybe not. All she cares about is my pay going into the bank. I'm merely a provider.'

There was no bitterness in the statement, just an overwhelming weariness, and Caroline knew that there was no way she could leave the stressed hospital manager in this state.

'I think that you both need to talk,' she advised gently. 'Maybe it would help if I went home with you and had a word with your wife. Does she know that you've been to see me?'

'No.'

'Well, then. It's time she did.'

She was drawing him away from the water and he gave a hollow laugh. 'I'm not going to throw myself in if that's what you're thinking, Dr Croft.'

'No, I'm sure you're not,' she said, 'but I do feel that your time would be better spent going home to talk to your wife, rather than staring into the lake.'

He sighed. 'It doesn't demand anything of me.'

'And she does?'

'All the time.'

'Maybe it only seems like that because you're so tired.'

'Huh! I'm that all right.'

'Yes, you are, and once the medication I've given you has had a chance to work things won't seem half so bad. So come along. I'll keep you company.'

'I believe you aren't aware that your husband has consulted me about the pressures of his job and how stressed and unwell he's feeling,' she said when a confident young blonde greeted them, stony-faced, at the Grices' home.

David Grice's wife stared at her blankly. 'No! He never said.'

'Maybe he didn't want to worry you, but it's clear that he recognised he needed help and your decision to leave him has increased his depression out of all proportion.'

'His mood swings are driving me mad,' she muttered, sinking onto the nearest chair.

In that moment she didn't seem smart, confident or anything else that was positive, and her husband moved slowly across to her and placed his arm around her shoulders.

'I know I've been difficult to live with lately,' he admitted, 'but it is only the job that's getting me down. I love you and the children just as much as I always have. Can't we try again?'

'I suppose so,' his wife agreed with a watery smile, and when Caroline saw the tension begin to lift she bade them a swift farewell. The Grices weren't the only ones with domestic problems to sort out, and hers had been put on hold for the last hour and a half.

'Where the dickens have you been?' Marcus said crossly when he opened the door to her. 'I thought we said half past eight!'

'Yes, we did,' she agreed apologetically, 'but I met a man in the park and I'm afraid I got sidetracked.'

'Sidetracked!'

'Er…yes. I'm afraid so.'

'Lennox, you mean?'

'John? No, of course not.'

'Well, whoever he was, it's quite clear that he was more congenial company than me. Maybe you should have stayed with him.'

She'd been about to explain how she'd found David Grice in a depressed state, but there was that same undertone to his manner that had been there before—the inference that she was unreliable.

With anger rising in her, Caroline eyed him levelly. 'Maybe I should, but it wasn't my company he needed. He was a patient in a distressed condition and my first priority was to get him away from the lakeside and back home.' As Marcus's face blanked in surprise she mounted her bicycle and rode off.

When they got out of their cars simultaneously on the deserted forecourt of the practice the next morning Caroline eyed Marcus coldly, but his response was pleasant enough and she thought achingly that the fact that he'd taken out his bad temper on her the previous night seemed to have been conveniently forgotten.

'We need to talk,' he said. 'I've booked a table for one o'clock at Mario's in the city centre, if that's all right with you?'

'Fish and chips in newspaper would do,' she said perversely. 'You don't have to try and get round me because you were completely insufferable last night.'

'With good reason,' he told her, his dark eyes glinting.

'Not from where I was standing. I was expecting an apology, but it appears that none is forthcoming. You should have known that, having said I'd come to you, I'd keep my word.'

'The invitation to dine with me this lunchtime was going to be in the form of an apology,' he said levelly, 'but as you appear to be impatient for the event to take place, here goes—an on-the-spot grovel.'

As she eyed him warily Marcus moved forward and took her firmly by the wrists. 'I'm sorry I was angry with you last night, Caroline,' he said smoothly, 'but sometimes you're a very elusive person.' His voice deepened. 'However, I've got you where I want you now so maybe it *is* a good time to kiss and make up.'

Her heart contracted. Not here it wasn't. Outside the practice in full view of passersby, and she wasn't sure that she wanted to 'kiss and make up', as he'd just described it. She was still hurting from last night.

'Let me go!' she snarled.

'All right,' he agreed, releasing her, 'but remember—one o'clock at Mario's. Yes?'

'Yes, if you say so,' she agreed frostily.

Caroline looked around her as an attentive waiter showed them to a table near the window. Mario's was a very elegant restaurant and she couldn't help wishing that they'd been dining there in the evening when she could have dressed to do justice to it, instead of partaking of lunch in her basic working attire.

But they were here because of last night's mix-up, not for a romantic rendezvous, and in a few moments they'd no doubt be crossing swords again, instead of discussing the wedding.

'Well?' he asked as they studied the menu.

Caroline looked up. 'Well, what?'

'Am I forgiven?'

'Would it make any difference if you weren't?'

'No, not really. My motives were honourable enough.'

She eyed him coldly. 'I'm not quite sure what you're referring to. Is it your bad temper of last night or your presumption of earlier this morning?'

'I'm talking about my bad temper of last night, as you describe it,' he said evenly, and before she could reply he went on with sudden gravity, 'I've been reluctant to mention this, but that fellow in the road-rage attack is still on the boil and has been making threats to me and mine because we got in his way.

'I had a warning phone call from the police just before you were due to arrive last night, and when you didn't appear my imagination was running riot.'

She began to smile. Maybe he really did care. But he'd have been anxious about anyone under those circumstances. So, instead of letting him see how much his concern meant to her, she said perversely, 'And were you intending to inform me of possible danger to myself and the children?'

Marcus sighed. 'Yes. I was going to tell you last night, but I was so swamped with relief to see you safe that I'd barely got my thoughts together before you went off in a huff.'

'And could you blame me?'

He stared at her across the table. 'For God's sake, Caroline! By the time you appeared I was incapable of coherent thought, but I wouldn't expect you to understand my feelings. That's not part of the package, is it?'

She wanted to tell him that a lot of things didn't look as if they were going to be part of the package, but she'd gone rigid in her seat.

Her eyes were fixed on the man and woman who'd just entered the restaurant. Totally engrossed in each other, her sister and John Lennox hadn't seen Marcus and herself until they were almost level with their table. As they gazed at the new arrivals in amazement Stephanie called out breezily, 'Hi, there.' Her companion acknowledged them with a quizzical lift of the eyebrows and then steered her sister to a table in the far corner.

'Maybe now you'll believe that there's nothing between John and me,' Caroline said in a stunned whisper when they'd gone past, 'because if they aren't a couple in love, I don't know who is!'

They were both silent on the way back to the practice, both occupied with their own thoughts, and it wasn't until he pulled up outside that Marcus said, 'I knew that Stephanie wasn't interested in me. She'd told me that she was in love with someone else, but I never dreamt it might be Lennox. How do you feel about it?'

'I'm delighted,' she said. 'Their temperaments will complement each other, although I remember Stephanie telling me when she first met him that my cadaverous friend wasn't her type. Obviously she was out to put me off the scent.

'But after that delightful surprise, let's get back to this business of the threats. Are we at risk, Marcus? It's a frightening thought.'

'The fellow is in custody as he has a previous record of violence,' he said soberly. 'He'll come before the magistrates today and could possibly go to prison for this.

'My paranoia last night was because I thought he might have someone who'd carry out his threats for him, such as family or friends, and when you'd gone steaming off on your bicycle I got in touch with the police again to make sure they were keeping an eye on your house.

'I've been in touch with them again this morning and it appears that he's calmed down now and is falling over himself to toe the line with the threat of prison hanging over him. So I think we can relax on that score, but I'll feel happier when our two families are joined and I can watch over you all at once. Think about it, eh, Caroline? The Owens and the Crofts as one invincible unit.'

The comment brought the wedding back to the forefront

of her mind once more and she didn't answer. Whenever that scenario surfaced, 'invincible' was the last thing she felt.

The next morning she was called out to the home of George and Margaret Bracken, a retired couple who lived in a small cottage in the shadow of the cathedral.

They were Geoffrey's patients, but as the senior partner wasn't there on Fridays the call had been passed on to Caroline.

The man who opened the door to her was big and in his youth must have been a striking figure. In some ways he still was, with a shock of thick white hair and twinkling blue eyes, but now the flesh hung loosely on him and his broad shoulders were stooped.

Although age had taken its toll of his body, his smile was brighter than the summer morning as he stepped back to let her in.

'It's my Margaret, Doctor,' he said as he led the way into a small, chintzy sitting room. 'She's got a really chesty cold and Dr Geoffrey has told us to send for him if anything like that develops because her movements are so restricted that it could soon turn to pneumonia.'

Caroline nodded gravely. 'Quite so, Mr Bracken. I take it that she's in bed?'

'Yes. The district nurse comes mid-morning to get her up for the day and I put her to bed at night.'

The patient's notes indicated that Margaret Bracken had suffered a stroke twelve months previously and it had left her with very little movement in her limbs. Mercifully her speech hadn't been affected, but her mobility was almost nil.

Extensive physiotherapy had been applied but with little effect. It had been suggested on several occasions that she go into care, but the man who was directing Caroline to a downstairs bedroom had refused to let her go, and as Caroline observed them together she understood why.

Margaret Bracken was tiny as her husband was large, but her smile was just as bright as his, and when he took her small hand tenderly in his big paw Caroline felt her throat tighten.

'It's the doctor to see you, Margaret,' he said gently, 'and it's a lady this time. If you remember, Dr Geoffrey isn't at the surgery on Fridays.'

His wife's laugh was a small tinkling sound. 'Yes, I know, dear. He's like us…getting old.' To Caroline, who was waiting with stethoscope at the ready to sound her chest, she said, 'I'm afraid that I'm a complete nuisance these days, Doctor. I don't know how George puts up with me.'

The man in question dropped to his knees and began to shuffle around the room on them, chuckling as he did so. 'Neither do I. As you can see, Doctor, I'm on my knees.'

'Get up, you old silly,' the woman in the bed said lovingly, 'or you'll be the next one that's incapacitated.'

'Not me,' he said stoutly as he brought himself upright again by holding onto the dressing-table. He winked in Caroline's direction. 'I'm indestructible.'

'Yes, I'm sure you are,' she agreed smilingly, only too aware of the tired lines around his eyes and the sparse gangling frame.

'Has Dr Geoffrey ever suggested a holiday for you both?' she asked, after sounding the sick woman's chest. 'There are places where your wife could be looked after while you have a rest.'

His face straightened. 'He did mention it once but we've been together fifty years, Doctor, and have never had a day apart. We're not going to start now.' He looked upwards. 'Not until that one up there says so, anyway.'

'I was meaning for you to both go to the same place,' she said patiently.

He brightened up immediately. 'Ah, now that's different…if we could be together.'

'Yes, of course you can,' she assured him, 'and once we've got this chest infection sorted out I'll ask Dr Geoffrey to work something out for you both. I'm going to prescribe antibiotics and a linctus and it should clear up in a few days. If it doesn't, give the practice another call.'

'George has to do so much for me. I worry about him a lot,' Margaret Bracken said. 'I'd go into a home but he won't agree to it.'

'No way,' he said staunchly. 'While there's breath in me, we stay together!'

'And when there isn't?' his wife asked gently.

'Then they'll have to get the bellows to me.' He chuckled.

CHAPTER ELEVEN

As CAROLINE drove back to the practice she was in a sombre mood. Occasionally in her life as a busy GP she came across a situation that had a thrall all of its own, and the love and devotion she'd just been privileged to witness at the Bracken house had been one of them.

There had been no bitterness about the circumstances they found themselves in, and their love for each other had been a humbling thing to witness. She envied them.

Tomorrow was her wedding day and it would be sadly lacking in the special sparkle that seemed to be kindled so easily in the lives of others.

You've known all along that was how it's going to be, she reminded herself, and don't forget that the boys are going to benefit by having Marcus around. But for the rest of the day her mood of melancholy persisted.

Marcus phoned that evening to check that all was well for the morrow. They'd seen little of each other during the day as he'd been out on calls, closeted with medical reps and then had spent the major part of the afternoon with the two locums who'd be filling in while they were on their honeymoon.

Finally, while she'd been coping with the afternoon surgery, he'd been called out to another suspicious death by the police. Desperate as she was for a few moments of his company, she'd eventually gone home unsatisfied.

'I'm sorry to have been so bogged down today,' he said when she picked up the phone. 'Thank God, we've got two whole weeks to ourselves to look forward to.'

At that particular moment Caroline felt incapable of looking forward to anything, and when there was silence at the other end of the line he said tautly. 'Is something the matter?'

'No,' she lied. 'I'm just tired. It's been a heavy day.'

'Tell me about it,' he agreed wryly, relief in his voice. 'So, are we all set for tomorrow?'

'Yes, I think so. The only thing I haven't been able to arrange is the weather.' *And my feelings with regard to what I'm about to do*, she wanted to cry.

'Good,' he said quickly, as if he'd been expecting something else. 'I think an early night is called for on both our parts, don't you? So that we'll be at our best for the big day.'

'Yes,' she agreed weakly. 'I think that's a good idea.' And with a listless farewell, she replaced the receiver.

Surprisingly she slept, but her slumbers were sluggish and dream-ridden and the moment Caroline opened her eyes to bright morning sunlight she knew what she had to do.

Throwing on an old pair of jeans and a crumpled T-shirt, she went to find Hetty and told the startled housekeeper, 'Don't let the boys and Stephanie start getting into the wedding outfits yet. I've got some thinking to do.'

'What!' Hetty cried, throwing up her hands in dismay. 'Surely you're not calling it off.' There was no answer forthcoming. Caroline had gone out through the open door, down the garden path and had disappeared from sight.

Her actions since she'd left her bed had been decisive and unswerving, but now, in the quiet, tree-lined road, she didn't know what to do or where to go.

All she knew was that she had to be by herself as she faced the dilemma she found herself in, and there was a deep sense of shame inside her because she'd been stupid enough to leave it this late, before facing up to it.

Marcus would be furious if she called the wedding off, but she consoled herself with the thought that it would be more hurt pride than the pain of real rejection that he'd feel. And surely he must have doubts of his own. But if he had, they hadn't been serious enough for *him* to have second thoughts.

As she walked on with slow dragging steps, Caroline found herself beside the cathedral. She looked up bleakly at its ancient stone perfection and it seemed to beckon her.

This was the place where she'd wanted to be married, she thought as the heavy wooden door swung to behind her and she stepped into its shadowed silence.

But she'd been divorced and it hadn't been possible. It was incredible how many things her marriage to Jamie had spoilt, the most important one being the chance of ever finding real love with Marcus. As misery engulfed her she groped her way to the nearest pew.

Sitting gazing blankly ahead, Caroline knew that from the moment of meeting Margaret and George Bracken the previous day this had been inevitable.

Not for anything—not for the twins' sake, not for little Hannah's sake and certainly not to gratify her longing to have Marcus on any terms—could she marry him unless she was sure. It would be a sin in the eyes of—

She heard the door slam to behind her but it didn't register. It was a sound coming from another world, a world that for a few desperate moments she'd shut out. But when she heard Marcus call her name she was hurtled back into it, mute with shock as she swung round to face him.

He was standing in a shaft of coloured light as the sun poured in through the stained-glass windows. It glinted on the dark gloss of his hair and revealed the mask of misery that was his face, and she got shakily to her feet.

'How did you know where to find me?' she quavered.

'Hetty followed you and then hurried back to phone me,' he said quietly. 'She seemed to think you were having doubts.'

'Yes. I am.'

'And were you going to do me the honour of informing me? Or was I to be left high and dry at the altar?'

She shook her head. 'No, of course not. It's still a couple of hours away. I would have let you know what I'd decided, but before I did I had to be by myself while I looked into my heart.'

'So you don't love me?'

Caroline felt her mouth drop open. Had she heard aright?

'It's the other way round,' she gasped. '*You* don't love me. I thought I could put up with less…but I can't!'

It was his turn to look amazed as he said raggedly, 'So you *do* care! I was prepared to accept whatever you felt you could give—it would have been better than nothing. But to know that you feel the same as I do is incredible. I *do* love you, Caroline. I always have. But you've kept me at arm's length ever since we met up again. Apart from letting me see that there was some sexual chemistry between us, you've never budged an inch.'

She couldn't believe she was hearing this. The day that had started so terribly was unfolding into something that she'd remember for ever.

'I've spent my life regretting leaving you,' she told him huskily, 'and when our paths crossed a second time it was as if I was being given a second chance. But then I realised that we were both wary of true commitment because we'd been scarred by unhappy marriages, even though we couldn't keep away from each other.

'When you asked me to marry you I accepted because I adore you and want to be with you, but yesterday it was brought home to me what real love is all about. I felt that what we had was second rate and that the kindest thing I could do was to call off the wedding.'

'Kind!' he cried. 'I nearly died when I got Hetty's phone call, and it wasn't because I was about to be jilted at the last moment. That didn't bother me at all. It was the thought of losing you that was driving me insane.'

His voice softened into tenderness and her bones melted at the tone. 'Come here, my beautiful woman,' he said softly, 'and let me tell you how much I love you. Believe me, it's far more than I ever cared for Kirstie.'

She stroked his face with gentle fingers. 'If you only knew how I've longed to hear you say that. I feel as if I've come in out of the wilderness.'

Marcus laughed deep in this throat. 'I'll say it again if you like...and again...and again.'

'Yes, please,' she whispered.

He looked around him at the stone aisles, worn smooth with many feet, the intricate carvings and ancient statues and the glorious windows that told the story of what the beautiful old church stood for. He said with a grin, 'I can't kiss the breath out of you in this place. It wouldn't be seemly. Let's go and tell Hetty and Stephanie that the bridesmaids' dresses and the pageboy outfits will be needed after all, shall we?'

'Yes! Oh, yes, indeed!' she cried, and hand in hand they walked out into the sunlight.

MILLS & BOON®

MEDICAL ROMANCE™

HER PASSION FOR DR JONES by Lilian Darcy
Southshore - No.1 of 4

Dr Harry Jones is sure it's a mistake having Rebecca Irwin work in the practice. Despite the raging attraction between her and Harry, Rebecca fought her corner!

BACHELOR CURE by Marion Lennox
Bachelor Doctors

Dr Tessa Westcott burst into Mike Llewellyn's life like a red-headed whirlwind. She said exactly what she thought, and turned his ordered world upside down. It couldn't last. But Mike had to admit, she lightened his life.

HOLDING THE BABY by Laura MacDonald

Lewis's sister was abroad and he was left holding the baby—literally! He *badly* needed help with the three children and asked Jo Henry to be nanny. In a family situation, Jo and Lewis became *vividly* aware of each other…

SEVENTH DAUGHTER by Gill Sanderson

Specialist registrar Dr James Owen was everything Dr Delyth Price ever wanted in a man. But Delyth had a gift not everyone understood. James seemed prepared to listen, if not to believe. Then she discovered his lighthearted side, and fell even deeper into love…

Available from 3rd September 1999

MILLS & BOON®

Next Month's Romance Titles

♡

Each month you can choose from a wide variety of romance novels from Mills & Boon®. Below are the new titles to look out for next month from the Presents...™ and Enchanted™ series.

Presents...™

A BOSS IN A MILLION	Helen Brooks
HAVING LEO'S CHILD	Emma Darcy
THE BABY DEAL	Alison Kelly
THE SEDUCTION BUSINESS	Charlotte Lamb
THE WEDDING-NIGHT AFFAIR	Miranda Lee
REFORM OF THE PLAYBOY	Mary Lyons
MORE THAN A MISTRESS	Sandra Marton
THE MARRIAGE EXPERIMENT	Catherine Spencer

Enchanted™

TYCOON FOR HIRE	Lucy Gordon
MARRYING MR RIGHT	Carolyn Greene
THE WEDDING COUNTDOWN	Barbara Hannay
THE BOSS AND THE PLAIN JAYNE BRIDE	Heather MacAllister
THE RELUCTANT GROOM	Emma Richmond
READY, SET...BABY	Christie Ridgway
THE ONE-WEEK MARRIAGE	Renee Roszel
UNDERCOVER BABY	Rebecca Winters

On sale from 3rd September 1999

H1 9908

Available at most branches of WH Smith, Tesco, Asda, Martins, Borders, Easons, Volume One/James Thin and most good paperback bookshops

Spoil yourself next month
with these four novels from

TEMPTATION

MACKENZIE'S WOMAN by JoAnn Ross

Bachelor Auction

Kate Campbell had to persuade Alec Mackenzie to take part in a
charity bachelor auction. This rugged adventurer would have
women bidding millions for an hour of his time. Trouble was,
Alec wasn't really a bachelor. Though nobody knew it—he was
married to Kate!

A PRIVATE EYEFUL by Ruth Jean Dale

Hero for Hire

Nick Charles was a bodyguard on a vital assignment. But no one
had yet told him exactly what that assignment was! So he was
hanging around a luxury resort, waiting… Then along came
luscious Cory Leblanc and Nick just knew she was a prime
candidate—for *something*…

PRIVATE LESSONS by Julie Elizabeth Leto

Blaze

'Harley' turned up on Grant Riordan's doorstep and sent his
libido skyrocketing. Hired as the 'entertainment' for a bachelor
party, she was dressed like an exotic dancer but had the eyes of
an innocent. Unfortunately, after a little accident, she didn't
have a clue who she was…

SEDUCING SYDNEY by Kathy Marks

Plain-Jane Sydney Stone was feeling seriously out of place in a
glamorous Las Vegas hotel, when she received a mysterious
note arranging a date—for that night! She was sure the message
must have been delivered to the wrong woman. But maybe
she'd just go and find out…

Our hottest

TEMPTATION

authors bring you...

Blaze

**Three sizzling love stories available in
one volume in September 1999.**

Midnight Heat
JoAnn Ross

A Lark in the Dark
Heather MacAllister

Night Fire
Elda Minger

FREE!

2 Books
and a surprise gift!

We would like to take this opportunity to thank you for reading this Mills & Boon® book by offering you the chance to take TWO more specially selected titles from the Medical Romance™ series absolutely FREE! We're also making this offer to introduce you to the benefits of the Reader Service™—

- ★ FREE home delivery
- ★ FREE gifts and competitions
- ★ FREE monthly Newsletter
- ★ Books available before they're in the shops
- ★ Exclusive Reader Service discounts

Accepting these FREE books and gift places you under no obligation to buy; you may cancel at any time, even after receiving your free shipment. Simply complete your details below and return the entire page to the address below. *You don't even need a stamp!*

YES! Please send me 2 free Medical Romance books and a surprise gift. I understand that unless you hear from me, I will receive 4 superb new titles every month for just £2.40 each, postage and packing free. I am under no obligation to purchase any books and may cancel my subscription at any time. The free books and gift will be mine to keep in any case.

M9EB

Ms/Mrs/Miss/Mr ....Initials.................................
BLOCK CAPITALS PLEASE

Surname..

Address..

....

....Postcode ....

Send this whole page to:
THE READER SERVICE, FREEPOST CN81, CROYDON, CR9 3WZ
(Eire readers please send coupon to: P.O. BOX 4546, KILCOCK, COUNTY KILDARE)